T0315320

J. R. R. Tolkien: A Very Short Introduction

VERY SHORT INTRODUCTIONS are for anyone wanting a stimulating and accessible way into a new subject. They are written by experts, and have been translated into more than 45 different languages.

The series began in 1995, and now covers a wide variety of topics in every discipline. The VSI library currently contains over 750 volumes—a Very Short Introduction to everything from Psychology and Philosophy of Science to American History and Relativity—and continues to grow in every subject area.

Very Short Introductions available now:

Available soon:

For more information visit our website

www.oup.com/vsi/

Matthew Townend

J. R. R. TOLKIEN

A Very Short Introduction

OXFORD
UNIVERSITY PRESS

OXFORD
UNIVERSITY PRESS

Great Clarendon Street, Oxford, OX2 6DP,
United Kingdom

Oxford University Press is a department of the University of Oxford.
It furthers the University's objective of excellence in research, scholarship,
and education by publishing worldwide. Oxford is a registered trade mark of
Oxford University Press in the UK and in certain other countries

Published in the United States of America by Oxford University Press
198 Madison Avenue, New York, NY 10016, United States of America

British Library Cataloguing in Publication Data

Data available

Library of Congress Control Number: 2024932740

ISBN 978-0-19-288204-2

Printed and bound by
CPI Group (UK) Ltd, Croydon, CR0 4YY

Contents

Acknowledgements

I am profoundly grateful to the many students at the University of York with whom, over the years, I have read and discussed Tolkien's works, and I would especially like to thank Joey Brooke, Rachel Brown, Rahul Gupta, Lillian Hammen, Katrine Hjulstad, and Yuki Kubota; I have learned a great deal from them. I am also deeply indebted to many previous writers on Tolkien, whose works have had a great influence on me: here, I would particularly like to acknowledge the inspiring scholarship of Tom Shippey, Wayne Hammond and Christina Scull, John Garth, and Dimitra Fimi.

For help and support in the writing and publication of this *Very Short Introduction*, I am grateful to Luciana O'Flaherty, Imogene Haslam, and Kripadevi Prabhakar at Oxford University Press, and Andrianna Marneros at HarperCollins. I am also grateful to Oxford University Press's anonymous readers for their corrections and suggestions. At home, I have been sustained by the love and companionship of my wife, Natasha Glaisyer, and our children, Robin and Kit. Finally, I would like to acknowledge a longstanding personal debt to the late Allan and Ellen Taylor, who gave me my first copy of *The Lord of the Rings* many years ago.

J. R. R. Tolkien

List of illustrations

Chapter 1
Reading Tolkien

J. R. R. Tolkien was the author of two of the most extraordinary, most original, and most popular books of the 20th century: *The Hobbit*, published in 1937, and *The Lord of the Rings*, published in 1954–5. He is a life-changing writer. The encounter with his works, and with *The Lord of the Rings* in particular, has had profound and far-reaching consequences for millions of readers, in altering their world-views, shifting their perspectives, and revealing new possibilities. For many readers, what they have experienced is a form of re-enchantment in the midst of the modern world: Tolkien's works have opened a door to the world of myth, folklore, and fairy tale, and to the discovery of what we now call fantasy literature (and the rediscovery of his Victorian predecessors). For some readers, an encounter with Tolkien's works has led to an environmental awakening. For others, a lifelong interest in languages—and in language in general—has been the result, including the languages and literatures of the Middle Ages. For yet others, the result has been a dedication to skills and crafts—calligraphy, perhaps, or cartography—or more communally a desire to enjoy and conserve the good things in life: friendship, storytelling, eating and drinking. For many, *The Lord of the Rings* has heightened their sense of justice for the overlooked or unimportant and has sharpened their distrust of the great and powerful. Some readers, perhaps, have even glimpsed the holy or numinous through Tolkien's works. And all this is in addition to enjoying two of the most exciting adventure stories written in the 20th century, both of which are poignant coming-of-age narratives, about the gains and losses that might occur in the movement from innocence to experience.

Every year, many people read *The Lord of the Rings* for the first time; but there are also many who read it (as hobbits would say) for the eleventy-first time. There can be very few books that have been reread as frequently and regularly as *The Hobbit* and (especially) *The Lord of the Rings*, and in the culture and practice of reading this is a peculiar phenomenon that is perhaps hard to parallel. It tells us something about the profundity of Tolkien's impact on many of his readers and the centrality that his writings assume in their life and mentality. Notoriously, in 1955, the anonymous reviewer in the *Times Literary Supplement* declared of *The Lord of the Rings* that 'this is not a work that many adults will read right through more than once'. As many commentators have since observed, it is hard to imagine a more spectacularly wrong judgement.

Tolkien is also a writer who has changed the common culture. Like The Beatles, say, or *Star Wars*, his work has permanently altered the forms and flavours of popular culture, at least in Europe and North America, and across several media, too: not just fiction, with the explosion of the fantasy genre that followed in his wake, but also music, gaming, and of course film and television. The release of Peter Jackson's three films of *The Lord of the Rings* (2001–3) extended the reach of Tolkien's world to new audiences and new generations, with Jackson's films of *The Hobbit* following in 2012–14. As a result, many readers now come to the books having seen the films first; but Tolkien's two great works had already assumed their positions of cultural impact long before the advent of the films. Tolkienian tropes and types are to be found everywhere in popular fantasy, from doughty dwarves and bow-wielding elves to halfling heroes and malevolent dark lords. Tolkien's imagination, like Dickens's in the 19th century or George

Orwell's in the 20th, has also proven to be myth-making as well as genre-making: few authors have created so many people or places that have since outgrown or escaped from the literary work in which they first appeared, to become recognizable icons with a life of their own, able to be used as a sort of communicative shorthand (for example, Gandalf, or Gollum, or Frodo, or Rivendell, or Mordor, all of which are often referenced in cultural or political contexts far removed from *The Lord of the Rings* itself).

He has also become a global phenomenon. In 2019, a fictionalized version of his own early life became the subject of a major film (called *Tolkien*), and in 2022, Amazon began broadcasting a multi-season television series *The Lord of the Rings: The Rings of Power*, set thousands of years before *The Hobbit* and *The Lord of the Rings* and with largely original content, for which overall costs are estimated in excess of $1 billion. What this indicates is that 'Tolkien' is now big business and a carefully managed brand or franchise, like Disney or Marvel, and is no longer simply the name of a single, very unusual author with his own quirks and quiddities. Inevitably, adaptations tend to diminish Tolkien's singularity in multifarious ways, as they reshape his work according to cultural norms—in addition to the changes in content and presentation that a transfer between media entails.

This *Very Short Introduction* will primarily examines the writer and his works, rather than his wider cultural impact or these more recent imaginings in other media. Naturally, it will give most prominence to *The Hobbit* and *The Lord of the Rings*, but it will also engage with the full range of Tolkien's writings, including his academic works and those posthumously published. It will seek to place Tolkien's works in the context of their composition, and it will take a thematic approach by exploring recurrent ideas and preoccupations in his writings, rather than reviewing his works one at a time in chronological order. It will give attention to those areas and concerns which Tolkien himself seems to have thought important, and to which his works have made a unique contribution, attempting to understand Tolkien on his own terms and in his own time. It will aim to be both informative and interpretative, providing both a compact guide for those in need of orientation and also, it is hoped, new ideas and insights for Tolkien cognoscenti.

Much of the pioneering scholarship on Tolkien was concerned with addressing and answering hostile judgements (or misjudgements) by some of his early critics. That situation has now largely passed, and there is less need for an agonistic approach. Not only does Tolkien continue to ride high on the bestseller lists, to generate multimillion dollar adaptations, and to stimulate a very great deal of fan-activity: he has also become a feature on university curriculums, alongside other 20th-century authors; and there are now journals, monographs, and multiple websites devoted to his life and works.

Hobbits, Tolkien wrote in the Prologue to *The Lord of the Rings*, 'liked to have books filled with things that they already knew, set out fair and square with no contradictions'. This may not be an ideal recipe for a *Very Short Introduction*: few subjects can have no contradictions or alternative points of view, and it is to be hoped that this book will not be entirely filled with things that its readers already know. But it will certainly endeavour to set out the nature of Tolkien's works and achievement as fairly and squarely as possible in the very short space available.

Chapter 2
Life and work

Biography

J. R. R. Tolkien was born on 3 January 1892. On many posthumous publications, and modern reprintings of his works, Tolkien's initials are prominently displayed on the cover or spine in a monogram of his own devising: JRRT. It can almost come as a shock to discover that he did, of course, have first names: John Ronald Reuel. To his wife and relatives, he was most commonly known as Ronald; to school friends, as John or John Ronald; and to friends in adulthood, often as Tollers. (Does 'Ronald Tolkien', as a name, give a different impression to 'J. R. R. Tolkien'?) Moreover, there is probably no major modern author whose name is so frequently misspelled: one finds the erroneous form 'Tolkein' repeatedly—a spelling as carelessly incorrect as, say, T. S. Elliot. There can also be uncertainty over its pronunciation, but Tolkien himself specified that his name should be pronounced *TOLL-keen* (with the stress on the first syllable and rhyming with *doll*).

He was born in the Orange Free State (now part of South Africa), in Bloemfontein. His parents were Arthur and Mabel Tolkien (born in 1857 and 1870, respectively), and he was their first child; two years later, the couple had a second son, Hilary. Arthur Tolkien was a bank manager, who had moved out to South Africa from England in 1889; Mabel joined him two years later, when they married. Although he could readily give an explanation of his unusual surname (he believed it to be derived from German *tollkühn*, 'foolhardy', though this is not certain), in his sense of self Tolkien seems to have placed more store by his mother's name and family—the Suffields, from Worcestershire.

In 1895, Mabel Tolkien returned to England with her two sons. Arthur was to have followed them, but he died in early 1896. The widowed Mabel began to build a new life for herself and her sons, in Sarehole near Birmingham, and the few years that followed seem to have been the happiest of Tolkien's childhood. He did not, however, acquire a Birmingham accent: later recordings attest to a form of Received Pronunciation or what was then called 'the King's English'.

Mabel Tolkien converted to Roman Catholicism in 1900, and as a result suffered various degrees of estrangement from her family. And then she died in 1904, from diabetes, leaving the young Ronald (aged 12) and Hilary (aged 10) as orphans. Because of Mabel's conversion, the two boys came under the guardianship of a Catholic priest, Father Francis Morgan of the Birmingham Oratory, and lived in a series of lodging houses, interspersed with stays with various relatives.

Tolkien was educated at King Edward's School, Birmingham. Here he made friends, played rugby, and prospered academically; and out of school he discovered the thrill of learning old languages, especially Germanic languages of the Middle Ages: Gothic, Old English, Old Norse. In 1911, having won an 'exhibition' or minor scholarship, he entered Exeter College, Oxford, to read Classics, but he subsequently changed his degree to English, graduating with a First in 1915.

While in lodgings in Birmingham in 1908, Tolkien had met another teenage orphan, Edith Bratt (born 1889), and the two fell in love. But on learning of the affair, Tolkien's guardian, Father

Francis, prohibited Tolkien from seeing Edith again until he reached the legal age of 21. They reunited in 1913 and married in 1916, and they had four children together: John was born in 1917, Michael in 1920, Christopher in 1924, and Priscilla in 1929.

At the start of the war in 1914, Tolkien had elected to press on and complete his undergraduate studies, but on graduation he joined the Lancashire Fusiliers as a Second Lieutenant. In June 1916, he was posted to the Western Front, to the Battle of the Somme, where he served as a signals officer. Of his three closest friends from school, two were killed in France. But in October 1916 Tolkien himself was invalided home with 'trench fever', and he never returned to front-line service: he spent the rest of the war in and out of hospitals, and his health seems never to have been especially robust after this (in 1923, for example, he nearly died of pneumonia).

The major traumas of Tolkien's life—the loss of his parents, his separation from Edith, his war service on the Somme, and the death of his friends—had all taken place before the age of 25. After that, his adult life, publicly at least, was decidedly uneventful—perhaps deliberately so, in reaction—though no doubt there were private crises and personal struggles that are not generally known, and we should not assume an untroubled existence: he later told one of his children that the outlet of his writing had 'stood [him] in good stead in many hard years'. (Tolkien's diaries and private letters have mostly remained the property of his family.)

After the First World War, Tolkien joined the staff of the *Oxford English Dictionary* and began tutoring for various Oxford colleges, and then in 1920 he and his family moved to Leeds, where he was appointed Reader (and later Professor) of English Language at the university. But they returned to Oxford in 1925, when, at the young age of 33, Tolkien became the Rawlinson and Bosworth Professor of Anglo-Saxon (a post associated with Pembroke College). And an Oxford professor he remained until his retirement in 1959, though he switched chairs in 1945 to become the Merton Professor of English Language. For thirty-five years he delivered lectures, examined and supervised students, and helped run the Faculty of English Language and Literature. His closest friend in Oxford, with a bond that was especially strong in the 1930s, was C. S. Lewis, then Fellow in English at Magdalen College; and Lewis and Tolkien were the two core members of the informal literary group known as the 'Inklings', who would gather once or twice a week to drink beer, read aloud their works-in-progress, and argue (or agree) about almost everything.

Upon his retirement from academia, Tolkien and his wife—their children now grown up—continued to live in Oxford, until they moved in 1968 to Bournemouth, where they had previously spent

1. J. R. R. Tolkien, *c.*1925.

a number of holidays. A crucial event in 1969—though it may not have seemed so at the time—was the sale of film rights to *The Hobbit* and *The Lord of the Rings*: this meant that, even decades later, control over film adaptations was no longer in the hands of his heirs and executors. Tolkien's wife Edith died in 1971; they had been married for fifty-five years. Tolkien returned to Oxford, to live in a flat provided by Merton College. He died on 2 September 1973, and the gravestone of Tolkien and his wife, in Wolvercote cemetery on the outskirts of Oxford, bears the names of Beren and Lúthien, characters in the love story that is one of the central tales in his Elvish mythology.

The man

What sort of a person was Tolkien? Many readers have, of course, formed something of their own impression from the experience of reading his works: Tolkien said that *The Lord of the Rings* was 'written in [his] life-blood', and before its publication he worried that he had 'exposed [his] heart to be shot at'. Any attempt to pin a personality in a few words must inevitably be reductive and possibly even disrespectful. But a number of character traits do emerge from the comments of those who knew Tolkien well or have studied him closely.

He was usually quite diffident: although he could grow animated in conversation, he seems to have felt no need, unlike C. S. Lewis, to shine in company. He was a dedicated and affectionate family man. He had a love of the natural world, expressed through botanical expertise and country walks. His political instincts were conservative, sometimes strongly so, but with a fascinating admixture of the liberal and even radical, and the adoption of *The Lord of the Rings* as an iconic text of the 1960s counter-culture perplexed him. He was a procrastinator and a perfectionist, a master of the displacement activity and a chronic non-finisher of tasks; and yet he wrote *The Lord of the Rings*. He was sociable and yet self-sufficient in many ways: Lewis thought him beyond influence in some regards, but Tolkien insisted he would never have completed or published *The Lord of the Rings* without Lewis's encouragement. Even after his book's great success, he continued to lack confidence in his work and to be anxious about 'expos[ing] my world of imagination to possibly contemptuous eyes and ears'. Like most people, he was complex and contradictory.

Humphrey Carpenter was appointed as Tolkien's authorized biographer after his death, with unique access to diaries and family papers. Carpenter gained the impression that Tolkien could be a man of both exuberant high spirits and also profound pessimism, perhaps even depression; and he traced this schism in his personality to the trauma of his mother's death. Carpenter also emphasizes humility as one of Tolkien's cardinal traits. On account of both his character and his Christian beliefs, he had a keen sense of the 'fallenness' of human beings—their weakness, susceptibility to temptation, and insufficiency—and he fully counted himself among those who were weak and inadequate.

Tolkien's consciousness of his own weakness, and his profound Catholic faith, led him to instincts of compassion and charity. Even as he thrilled to stories of heroism and adventure, at the same time his sympathies tended to be not so much with the great and lofty as with the little people involved—literally as well as metaphorically. He emerged from the First World War with a sense of his own inferiority in terms of courage and endurance, and it is in his invention and celebration of hobbits—their culture, character, and world-view—that Tolkien's instincts and sympathies are arguably most fully expressed. He remained distrustful of power and of the effects of power on even the well intentioned.

Viewed externally, Tolkien's life may look conventional and perhaps even stuffy—close to the stereotype of the tweedy Oxford don. Fair-haired and slight of build, most photos show him formally attired, in well-tailored suits and jackets, with a hint of dressiness. But assured appearances can be misleading, and a number of life-circumstances had led Tolkien, in spite of his thirty-five years in the Oxford professoriate, to retain a sense of himself as something of an outsider and a warm sympathy for other outsiders. He had been an orphan, a grammar school boy, and a poor undergraduate. He was the first in his immediate family to go to university, and two of his main scholarly mentors were Joseph Wright and Henry Bradley, both working-class autodidacts. His wife Edith was illegitimate. He was a colonial, someone born in South Africa rather than England; and as with many veterans, his experience in the Great War seems to have led to a certain alienation from the rest of society. Perhaps most importantly, he felt an enduring sense of prejudice and discrimination against Catholics.

So this conventional-looking don was not so conventional after all—quite apart from the astonishing imagination that was teeming within him.

The scholar

Before we turn to his creative writings, however, we must attend to Tolkien's professional activities. His main duties, both at Leeds and Oxford, lay in the teaching of medieval language and literature: at one time or another, he taught Old English (Anglo-Saxon), Middle English, Old Norse, Gothic, and other Germanic and also Celtic languages, with the first three forming the core of his teaching. But Tolkien didn't usually call himself a 'medievalist' or a scholar of English; instead, the term he preferred was 'philologist', and his discipline was 'philology'.

The term (and the discipline) is now rather neglected or forgotten, but in the 19th century, philology—literally, 'the love of words'—formed one of the great historicist enterprises of the age. Pioneered in Germany and Denmark, philology took root in

Britain from the mid-century onwards. Just as revolutions in geology brought about a new understanding of the history of the Earth, with an emphasis on change over time, and evolutionary biology did the same for the natural world, so 19th-century philology marked a paradigm shift in the study of language: it emphasized the importance of historical study, with language itself becoming the object of attention rather than simply a means or medium for studying other things; it took a comparative approach, ranging across national boundaries and reconstructing earlier language-states not preserved in extant sources; and it foregrounded spoken language over written, viewing the former as primary and the true location of language.

But philology was not simply what we would now call historical linguistics. It had a wider historical ambition too, seeing language as the key to unlocking past cultures; it thus had close affinities with other Victorian disciplines such as manuscript studies, folklore, and anthropology. This was Tolkien's professional field and the core of his intellect and sensibility, though he did not make overvalued claims for its importance or think it 'necessary to salvation'.

At the end of his career, Tolkien wrote that he 'would always rather try to wring the juice out of a single sentence, or explore the implications of one word than try to sum up a period in a lecture, or pot a poet in a paragraph'. Much of his scholarly activity was concerned with the making of editions, either for publication or for teaching purposes, and his undergraduate lectures often involved him working through set texts in linear order, passage by passage and crux by crux, offering brilliant insights as he did so. (A number of these commentaries have been posthumously published.) But he did engage in some poet-potting and summing up of periods, above all in two of his most influential publications, '*Beowulf*: The Monsters and the Critics' (published 1937) and 'On Fairy-Stories' (published 1947). The first of these, with persuasive rhetoric and in argument with his academic forebears, insisted that the great Old English poem *Beowulf* should be read with appreciation of its status as a poem and not simply as a repository of historical traditions; the second tried to characterize and theorize the value of folktales and fairy tales.

Both of these pieces took the form of long articles; and the long article seems to have been the limit of what Tolkien was able to achieve on his own. With his Leeds collaborator E. V. Gordon he produced a landmark edition of the Middle English poem *Sir Gawain and the Green Knight* (1925), but all of Tolkien's other annotated editions, such as that of the poem *The Wanderer* for Methuen's Old English Library, failed to reach completion; and some of them sat on his desk for years (or, in the case of the *Clarendon Chaucer*, for decades), never quite being brought to a state of finish. Nor did Tolkien ever publish an academic monograph or book-length study, as might have been expected. He made a number of translations—for example, of *Beowulf*, *Pearl*, and *Sir Gawain and the Green Knight*—but again these failed to reach print during his lifetime.

Although in his youth he had a taste for amateur theatricals, in his professional life he was regarded as a poor lecturer. When Tolkien's fame began to grow, after *The Lord of the Rings*, a number of former pupils or audience members gave their reminiscences: while for W. H. Auden Tolkien's *Beowulf* lectures were an 'unforgettable experience' ('the voice was the voice of Gandalf', he wrote), Kingsley Amis, more typically, recalled Tolkien's lectures as being 'incoherent and often inaudible'. Tolkien's influence on his field came in two main ways: first, through his key articles (small in number but highly significant), and second, through his supervision of PhD students, many of whom went on to distinguished academic careers, and who published in their own works ideas which they had first developed with Tolkien. Such former students often felt great loyalty and affection for him: Robert Burchfield, who became editor of the *Oxford English Dictionary*, looked back gratefully to this 'puckish fisherman who drew me into his glittering philological net'.

Over time, though, Tolkien seems to have acquired a reputation for laziness at Oxford, on account of his failure to publish major academic works. So, for example, although his brilliance as a scholar was universally recognized, Tolkien was never, unlike C. S. Lewis, elected as a Fellow of the British Academy—a sign, perhaps, of the ambivalence with which his peers viewed the sum of his academic achievements. Did they feel that he had not quite fulfilled his potential?

We know from various records that Tolkien was not lazy: he took his duties very seriously, as lecturer, supervisor, examiner, and administrator. But at the same time there is no doubt that he sat on things: he failed to complete his own work, and he delayed in the return of other people's. In particular, during his tenure of the Merton chair (1945–59) his academic productivity was minimal: he published almost nothing, and at this point in his career, as opposed to in earlier decades, it is hard not to conclude that this is because much of the time available for research (especially in university vacations) was being devoted to his creative writing instead.

Because what he did complete and prepare for publication during this time were the three volumes of *The Lord of the Rings*, in 1954 and 1955—which in turn generated much new writing and new correspondence. Of course, it seems uncontroversial to say that, in the grand scheme of things, Tolkien's writing of *The Lord of the Rings* has contributed infinitely more to human happiness and understanding than any number of articles on Old and Middle English would have done; nonetheless, it is hard to deny that he was employed to produce advanced research, and as he himself later acknowledged, he had committed 'crimes of omission' in order to finish his great work.

In a pioneering study, Tom Shippey characterized Tolkien's characteristic method as an imaginative writer as 'creation from philology'. This is absolutely right; but the formula can also be reversed, and we can say that Tolkien practised philology from, or by means of, creation. In other words, many of Tolkien's scholarly insights were often articulated not in the traditional academic form of an edition or article but rather in a poem or story.

In some cases, Tolkien's creative work cleaves quite closely to the medieval text or philological problem to which it was a response: his long poems on Sigurd and Gudrún represent Tolkien's attempt to make sense of the contradictions and absences in the heroic poems of the Old Norse *Edda*; his short story *Sellic Spell* is a reconstruction of the folktale archetype that may have underlain the figure of Beowulf; and his verse drama *The Homecoming of Beorhtnoth Beorhthelm's Son* is an extended meditation on the Old English poem *The Battle of Maldon*. Tolkien's study of Arthurian texts led to his alliterative poem *The Fall of Arthur*; his interest in Breton *lais* resulted in *The Lay of Aotrou and Itroun*; and so on. But in many other cases, Tolkien's scholarly ideas, the fruit of much thought and learning, are embedded in more piecemeal and submerged fashion in his works of Middle-earth.

A literary life

In a number of end-of-millennium polls, *The Lord of the Rings* was repeatedly acclaimed as the 'Book of the Century'. These were serious-minded surveys: other high-ranking works included James Joyce's *Ulysses* and George Orwell's *Nineteen Eighty-Four*. But Tolkien's biography hardly conforms to our usual ideas of what the life of a major 20th-century author should look like. Most obviously, Tolkien was not a professional writer. He earned his living through university teaching, not creative writing, and he did his own writing in his own time—effectively as a hobby, like an amateur painter or maker of model boats, however seriously he may have taken it and however congruent it may have been with his professional concerns. Nor was he much connected with the literary world of publishers, periodicals, and prizes: he didn't write book reviews or engage in controversies, and he only became a public figure in his seventies, when *The Lord of the Rings* became a sensation. And the success of *The Lord of the Rings* was itself a reader-led, word-of-mouth phenomenon, not the result of a media campaign: Tolkien's publishers were uncertain that the work would break even, and it received little support from prominent cultural arbiters. If Tolkien's works have been 'canonized', this has been a movement from below, by millions of readers.

His career as a writer is also atypical in terms of his publication history. The list of creative works (book-length, single-authored) that he published during his lifetime is very short, as follows:

1937	*The Hobbit*
1949	*Farmer Giles of Ham*
1954–5	*The Lord of the Rings*
1962	*The Adventures of Tom Bombadil*
1964	*Tree and Leaf*
1967	*Smith of Wootton Major*

In effect, Tolkien published two major works; the other four items in this list are all quite minor. (*The Lord of the Rings* is one book, published in three volumes; it is not a trilogy.) Moreover, the dates of publication are misleading in terms of indicating Tolkien's biography as a writer. *The Hobbit* was probably mostly written in the period 1929–32. The main writing of *The Lord of the Rings* extended from 1937 to 1948; the years after that were devoted to revision, retyping, and preparing for publication. The first versions of *Farmer Giles of Ham* were written in the late 1920s and early 1930s. *The Adventures of Tom Bombadil* is a collection of mostly pre-existing poems, some of which had been written as far back as the 1920s. *Tree and Leaf* was a reprinting of two earlier works (*Leaf by Niggle* and 'On Fairy-Stories'), which had originally been published in 1945 and 1947. Only the brief *Smith of Wootton Major* was published soon after it was written.

Thanks to a remarkable programme of posthumous publication and curatorial care, mostly undertaken by Tolkien's son Christopher (above all in his twelve-volume 'History of Middle-earth', 1983–96), we now know that Tolkien's published works formed only a modest portion of a truly prodigious quantity of creative writings. If we place the most significant posthumously published works in sequence not of publication but of likely or approximate date of composition, we get a much better sense of Tolkien's development as a writer (the following list is confined to major works, and dates are taken from Christina Scull and Wayne G. Hammond's authoritative *J. R. R. Tolkien Companion and Guide*):

1916–20	*The Book of Lost Tales*
1919–25	*The Lay of the Children of Húrin*
1925–31	*The Lay of Leithian*
1927	*Roverandom*
late 1920s/early 1930s	*Mr Bliss*
1930	*Quenta* (or *Qenta*) *Noldorinwa*
early 1930s	*The New Lay of the Volsungs* and *The New Lay of Gudrún*
early 1930s	*The Fall of Arthur*
1930s	*Quenta Silmarillion* and *Annals*
1936–7	*The Lost Road* and *The Fall of Númenor*
1945–6	*The Notion Club Papers*
early 1950s	*Of Tuor and His Coming to Gondolin*
1950s	*Narn i Chîn Húrin* and *The Wanderings of Húrin*
1950s	*Quenta Silmarillion* and *Annals* (revised and enlarged)
late 1950s	*Athrabeth Finrod ah Andreth*
late 1950s	*Laws and Customs among the Eldar*
late 1950s	*Quendi and Eldar*
early 1960s	*Aldarion and Erendis*

One might expect such an abundance of unpublished works to survive only as first drafts. But in fact, many of Tolkien's unpublished writings exist in multiple manuscript and typescript versions, indicating several stages of revision and polish; this is not simply a catalogue of false starts. But most of these works, even though they exist in multiple versions, are indeed unfinished. Clearly, Tolkien had as much difficulty in completing his major creative works as he did his academic ones. Composition proceeded in a distinctive rolling fashion: he rarely waited till he got to the end of a work before going back to the start and embarking on a new revision, and then once again failing to get to the end; hence the proliferation of different, incomplete versions. He also kept putting writings down and then picking them up again, so that composition could extend over a great length of time. Many writings were only eventually published (or abandoned) years or even decades after they were first begun: there can be few other authors for whom dates of publication offer such a fundamentally unreliable guide to the chronology of their writing career. Tolkien didn't simply write a book, publish it, and then move on to the next one. A further consequence of the high proportion of posthumously published works in Tolkien's total oeuvre is that many details, both narrative and conceptual, must be regarded as non-definitive—the record of evolving or even fleeting ideas rather than a final, settled position. Unpublished writings do not necessarily bear the same status as works authorially prepared for publication.

Nonetheless, if we look at these timelines, we can gain some sense of the shape of Tolkien's history as a writer. The writing of poetry was a constant, but the first major work he embarked on was the prose *Book of Lost Tales*—his first sustained attempt to tell what later became known as the mythology of the 'Silmarillion'. In the 1920s, when his children were young and his academic career was most demanding, he wrote long narrative poems (continuing also, in alliterative verse, into the early 1930s). In the late 1920s and early 1930s, Tolkien also began to compose longer written stories for his children; and *The Hobbit* is a product of this period. In the 1930s, Tolkien also spent much time on the various texts of the

'Silmarillion'. This progress was interrupted by the publication of *The Hobbit* and then the writing of *The Lord of the Rings*. But after the drafting of his great work was complete, and even before it was published, he returned to his 'Silmarillion' stories with renewed vigour. But the effort was again frustrated, being undermined by Tolkien's own doubts about his mythology, interrupted by the demands brought by fame, and increasingly affected by old age and poor health for both himself and his wife. Attempts to finish and publish the 'Silmarillion' as a book, or as a collection of texts, were unsuccessful, even though the work was eagerly awaited; and Tolkien's creative career, in his final years, came to an end with a series of essays and notes as he tried to puzzle out what he saw as problems in his mythological writings.

This is a very unusual literary career. There was nothing at all inevitable about Tolkien's eventual acclaim as a writer, and it is easy to imagine ways in which his life as a writer (and, therefore, our knowledge of his writings) might have gone very differently. So, for example, having written *The Hobbit*, a book of dazzling originality, Tolkien seems to have made no attempt to publish it. In the years following its composition, the typescript of *The Hobbit* was lent out to various friends for private reading, until by a roundabout route it came to the attention of Susan Dagnall, an Oxford English graduate who now worked for the London publisher George Allen and Unwin—and the rest, as it were, is history. Allen and Unwin asked Tolkien to tidy up the text and prepare illustrations; and the book appeared in September 1937, thus marking the real beginning of Tolkien's career as a published writer (aged 45).

The Lord of the Rings was then written directly in response to Allen and Unwin's request for a sequel to *The Hobbit*, and its completion is the central miracle of Tolkien's career. He was well aware of this, calling it 'the chief biographical fact' of his life as a writer, and continuing to be 'astonishe[d]' by it. Somehow, after a stop–start composition process that lasted over a decade, and at a point in late middle age when he was already well set in his ways, this serial non-finisher of projects managed to bring his 500,000-word story to completion—and then see it through the press. Without *The Lord of the Rings*, we would now most likely remember Tolkien as the one-book author of *The Hobbit*, a children's classic whose merit was immediately recognized on publication (it was nominated for the 1937 Carnegie Medal, losing out to Eve Garnett's *The Family from One End Street*). But it was *The Lord of the Rings* that changed the world—the unplanned, unexpected masterpiece of a very unlikely 'author of the century'.

Chapter 3
Stories

Trying to find out

Tolkien was above all a storyteller. His first instinct was usually to proceed via narrative rather than analysis and argument—though the analysis and argument often followed afterwards.

Tolkien's whole career as a mythological writer effectively began in 1914. Fascinated by the word (or name) *earendel* in the Old English poem *Christ II*, in the September of that year he wrote a narrative poem, 'The Voyage of Earendel the Evening Star'. This was the beginning of what would grow into his 'Silmarillion' mythology and would occupy the rest of his life. But when, at the time of composition, a friend asked him what the poem was about, Tolkien replied: 'I don't know. I'll try to find out.'

In one of the most famous origin stories in modern literature, Tolkien recalled that one summer a decade and a half later, when marking examination scripts, he scribbled on an empty page, seemingly out of nowhere: 'In a hole in the ground there lived a hobbit.' But this moment of inspiration, giving the first sentence of *The Hobbit* and a new, invented word, was not to be fully worked out—scrutinized, historicized, and theorized—until more than twenty years later, on the final page of the appendices to *The Lord of the Rings*. Here, Tolkien told his readers both that the word *hobbit* is really—or so he claimed—a translation of the 'Westron' word *kuduk* (earlier *kûd-dûkan*) meaning 'hole-dweller', and that its modern English form is derived from an Old English original *holbytla*, also meaning 'hole-dweller'. These detailed claims were all fictions or after-the-event justifications, invented by Tolkien himself—but he evidently thought them necessary for reasons of consistency and verisimilitude.

In both small matters and great, this was a characteristic mode of creative advance for Tolkien. No doubt for many writers and artists a distinction might be made between the idea or moment of inspiration and the later working out of that idea; but for Tolkien these two forms of creativity—the story-making and the system-making—were unusually distinguishable, and the relationship between the two was unusually productive. Some of his works, or sections of his works, are marked by a high quotient of the inspirational or story-making; others are almost wholly comprised of system-making rationalizations. So, for example, a number of figures who are mysterious and unexplained in *The Hobbit*—such as Gollum and Beorn—later receive explicatory back stories in *The Lord of the Rings*. The appendices to *The Lord of the Rings* themselves explain many matters that are cryptic or allusive in the main body of the story. And other figures who sprang into life in the writing of *The Lord of the Rings* then had to be woven into the 'Silmarillion'.

In many respects, this is the tension between storytelling and world-building. There are pleasures to be had from both forms of creation, of course, for both writer and reader, as Tolkien himself was well aware; but they are not the same and may even be in competition with each other. As Tolkien grew older, his inclination seems to have been increasingly towards the explanatory and system-making—one of a number of reasons why he was unable to complete the 'Silmarillion' as an integrated work. But some figures, perhaps thankfully, remained unexplained: Tom Bombadil is a supreme example.

The same bifurcation, viewed from a different angle, can be seen in Tolkien's critical remarks about his own works. His proclaimed aversion to allegory is well known ('I cordially dislike allegory in all its manifestations', he announced in the foreword to the second edition of *The Lord of the Rings*); but it is unquestionable that some of his works are allegorical in either a strict or a loose sense—most obviously *Leaf by Niggle*, the story of an artist unable to complete his painting. It is as if the inspired creator of the works, and the literary-critical self-commentator, are two different people, with the latter seemingly failing to recognize one of the key ways in which the former's writings possess power. Tolkien's late tale *Smith of Wootton Major* beautifully distils the essence of Faërie, and the sense of Faërie's allure and enchantment to ageing mortals. The story is delicate, suggestive, and freighted with sadness and meaning. But then, after its composition, Tolkien wrote a long essay about his story, and this heavy-handed analysis seems strangely to misconstrue what sort of tale it is, treating it in the manner of a documentary history (with a rigorous focus on questions of chronology, social history, and economics).

This tension between story-making and system-making, between narrative and world-building, was for Tolkien one of the mainsprings of his creativity; others, to be discussed in Chapters 5 and 6, included his relations with earlier literary works and the generative power of language. But the goal of the present chapter is to review Tolkien's activities as a storyteller, and so we will now turn to his major works in sequence.

The 'Silmarillion' (1)

The 'Silmarillion' is the name usually given to the body of myths and legends which Tolkien worked on for nearly sixty years—from its beginnings in 1914 until his death in 1973. It was a private mythology of lifelong fascination and ever-increasing complexity. The stories of the 'Silmarillion' are set in the so-called Elder Days, the period later to be labelled, in the chronology of *The Lord of the*

Rings, as the First Age, and the placing of the title in inverted commas (the 'Silmarillion') is normally done to distinguish the sprawling, multi-decade corpus of unpublished writings from the selective, editorially tidied version that Christopher Tolkien published as *The Silmarillion* in 1977 after his father's death. Subsequently, Christopher Tolkien published most of the earlier, constitutive writings within the multi-volume 'History of Middle-earth', of which two-thirds of the contents are 'Silmarillion'-related.

What we now call the 'Silmarillion', then, was in Tolkien's lifetime an ever-evolving body of material, which means that it is difficult to summarize its narrative contents, and also that—since Tolkien kept changing many details, from names to plot elements—any summarizing account must of necessity combine features from different periods.

But at its heart, the 'Silmarillion' tells the story of the Elves. It begins at a cosmological scale, in which Ilúvatar (Tolkien's deity) brings the world into being through the music of the Ainur or Valar (who are called 'gods' in the earliest versions but are later redesignated as 'powers'). But one of the Valar, named Melko(r) or Morgoth, rebels against Ilúvatar and endeavours to conquer and subdue the created world to his will. The 'Silmarillion' tells of the awakening of the Elves, and of how some of them journeyed to Valinor, home of the Valar on the western landmass of Aman, while others remained on the eastern landmass of the 'Great Lands' or (later) 'Middle-earth'. Light is given to the world through the Two Trees of Valinor, and Fëanor, the greatest craftsman of the Elves, captures the light of the Trees in three jewels known as Silmarils. But Morgoth kills the trees and steals the Silmarils, and much of the 'Silmarillion' then tells of the long wars fought back in Middle-earth between Morgoth and the Elves (and later 'Men' too, as Tolkien called humans in his mythology). In the end, the Valar intervene, and in the defeat of Morgoth some of the lands of Middle-earth, known as Beleriand, are broken and reshaped.

Embedded in this grand narrative are a number of individual stories which are treated at greater length, in particular the three 'great tales' of Beren and Lúthien (two lovers who recover a Silmaril from Morgoth's iron crown), Túrin Turambar (an ill-fated warrior and dragon-slayer), and the Fall of Gondolin (the last Elvish city to hold out against Morgoth). A fourth great tale, never written, was to be that of Earendel or Eärendil, the mariner who, at the end of the cycle, seeks help from the Valar and finally sails into the heavens with a Silmaril bound to his brow.

The Christian parallels, or presuppositions, of Tolkien's mythology are plain enough. There is one omnipotent deity, who brings the world and its inhabitants into existence though an act of creation; there is a subordinate body of supreme or perhaps angelic beings (the Ainur, subdivided into the Valar and the lesser Maiar); and there is a Satan equivalent in the figure of Morgoth. The peoples ranged against Morgoth, again according to Christian assumptions, are not free from flaws by any means: the Elves of the 'Silmarillion' are divided into factions and often suspicious of others, while Fëanor and his sons are driven to kin-slaying and other misdeeds through their desire to recover the Silmarils. The 'Silmarillion' is unclassifiable: it is myth, theology, history, epic, cosmology, and tragedy all in one.

And in its beginnings, it was fairy tale too. Tolkien's first telling was in elevated, archaic prose, in *The Book of Lost Tales*, begun during the First World War. The *Lost Tales* were structured as a story-collection with a frame narrative, in which a wanderer comes to an isle of the Elves and learns their history: the stories reveal the young Tolkien as a romantic and a fairy-tale enthusiast, and not yet either the systematic world-builder or elegiac moralist of subsequent years. But they also demonstrate how some of Tolkien's recurrent iconography, familiar to his readers from his later works, was present from the very beginning: the stories in *The Book of Lost Tales* feature trees, towers, jewels, dragons, spiders, and eagles, as well as a host of other motifs and properties. Then, in the 1920s, Tolkien recast two of the great tales into poetry: the story of Túrin Turambar became 2,000 lines of alliterative verse (*The Lay of the Children of Húrin*), and that of Beren and Lúthien 4,000 lines of rhyming couplets (*The Lay of Leithian*). But like the *Lost Tales* before them, neither of these poems was completed.

An important new form evolved almost by accident. In 1926, Tolkien wrote a 'Sketch of the Mythology' as a background guide for a reader of his Túrin lay. This compact digest, free of the frame narrative, the dialogue, and the dramatic storytelling of *The Book of Lost Tales*, was in turn expanded into the more polished *Quenta Noldorinwa* of 1930 (which, uniquely among these successive versions, was finished)—which was itself then revised into the incomplete *Quenta Silmarillion*, and then abandoned when Tolkien turned to *The Lord of the Rings*. In the 1930s, this new digest tradition was also accompanied by a recasting of the contents of the mythology into annalistic shape, in the *Annals of Valinor* and the *Annals of Beleriand*, and a variety of other forms too. In the 1920s and 1930s, Tolkien also drew maps and painted pictures to illustrate his mythology.

These evolving forms of the 'Silmarillion' demonstrate Tolkien's inclination to tell the same stories over and over again—above all, in the multiple versions of the tale of Túrin Turambar—and also his increasing preference for a mode of narrative that was far removed from anything that might be regarded as novelistic. The mythology also continued to ramify: the 1930s saw the first versions of the Atlantis-like myth of Númenor, a new direction which focused on Men rather than Elves and which took the chronology forwards beyond the Elder Days, into what would later be called the Second Age.

Perhaps we can imagine an alternative history in which Tolkien did complete and publish a version of his 'Silmarillion' mythology in the 1920s or 1930s (*The Book of Lost Tales*, say, or the *Quenta*

Silmarillion). With its remote content and elevated style, it is hard to imagine such a work having mass appeal, and Tolkien's literary reputation—if we imagine *The Hobbit* as never having reached Allen and Unwin—would now more likely be as a niche author of early 20th-century fantasy or heroic romance. Or maybe Tolkien would never have published his stories at all, and they would have remained a private endeavour, known only to a few friends and family: he was well aware of this possibility himself, imagining a future (in the fictional *Notion Club Papers*) in which the manuscript of a work called *Quenta Eldalien, being the History of the Elves, by John Arthurson* ends up languishing in a second-hand bookshop in Oxford. In Tolkien's career as an author, it was the creation of hobbits that made him and saved him, as they generated an audience for his writings, reconfigured the grandeur of myth through their humour and homeliness, and directed their inventor's imagination towards new endeavours.

The Hobbit

The Hobbit began as one of a number of works which Tolkien composed for his children in the late 1920s and late 1930s; the earliest version of *Farmer Giles of Ham*, for example, begins, 'Then Daddy began a story, and this is what he said', and these were also the golden years for the 'Father Christmas letters' which Tolkien wrote annually for his children. Without one central root being his family storytelling, Tolkien's fiction would likely have developed very differently. *The Book of Lost Tales*, and the earlier apprentice piece *The Story of Kullervo*, show us the kind of writing that Tolkien aspired to before he had children: tales composed in a high, archaic style, and often tragic and stern in content. These two disparate elements achieve their creative symbiosis in *The Lord of the Rings*. But after his great work had been finished and published, and his children had grown up, Tolkien did not write any more stories for children, or any more tales about hobbits, almost as if *The Hobbit* and *The Lord of the Rings* had been an intrusion or aberration.

The Hobbit tells the story of the unadventurous Bilbo Baggins, who is catapulted out of his comfortable home in Hobbiton by the wizard Gandalf and a band of dwarves led by Thorin Oakenshield, to aid them in their quest to defeat the dragon Smaug and regain the dwarves' old kingdom at the Lonely Mountain. After many adventures on the journey (trolls, goblins, spiders, and more), Bilbo finds himself obliged to creep down into the heart of the mountain to steal a treasure from Smaug's hoard. The story ends with the killing of Smaug by the archer Bard of Lake-town, the Battle of Five Armies in which the dwarves' enemies are defeated but Thorin is mortally wounded, and Bilbo's journey back home to discover that he has lost his good standing in Hobbiton: the narrator reports that he subsequently 'took to writing poetry and visiting the elves'.

Tolkien's two most famous works are written in very different literary modes. In gaining a clear view of *The Hobbit* in particular, it is important not to back-project onto it the contents and manner of the later *Lord of the Rings*. The world of *The Hobbit*, for example, is never called 'Middle-earth', and Bilbo's home is never called 'the Shire'. The Lonely Mountain is never 'Erebor'. Indeed, notwithstanding occasional references to Gondolin and 'the High Elves of the West' (and similar allusions are also found in the children's story *Roverandom*), it is not certain whether *The Hobbit* was originally intended as being part of the 'Silmarillion' mythology or not. Designation of the world of the story as 'the Northern world' or simply 'the North' suggests that the story was intended as being set, recognizably, in the same lands as early medieval legend. It was only the writing of *The Lord of the Rings* which joined together the worlds of *The Hobbit* and the 'Silmarillion' into one coordinated history.

The Hobbit is a children's story and often viewed as one of the last great contributions to the so-called 'Golden Age of Children's Literature'. Its influence on later children's fiction is immense, and it has been formative both for the 20th-century association between fantasy and children's literature and also for the miscategorization of Tolkien as fundamentally a children's writer. The narrator's tone of voice and manner of address is obviously that of an adult speaking to a child audience ('Now you know enough to go on with')—though the prominence of this sort of writing, which Tolkien later came to regret, declines as the story proceeds. Although he is an adult hobbit, Bilbo is a proxy child within the narrative: the story tells of his discovery of the world beyond his home and of his growth and maturation as an independent actor.

He is also a proxy for the reader within the text. The world into which Bilbo is plunged is archaic, heroic, and filled with alien conventions and patterns of behaviour. But Bilbo himself is unmistakably modern, both in his material culture and his sensibilities, and he thus acts as a mediating device for the modern (originally inter-war) reader. This role for hobbits as intermediaries would be taken further in *The Lord of the Rings*; here, Bilbo is a kind of anachronistic interloper into the legendary northern world, with his creature comforts, middle-class squeamishness, and post-medieval ideas and clothing (the heroes of old did not, of course, wear waistcoats or possess trousers with pockets).

We can also view *The Hobbit* as an extended fairy tale. Populated with creatures from folklore, and furnished with plot-turning artefacts such as rings and keys, *The Hobbit* repeatedly positions itself, especially in its early chapters, by reference to some of the familiar tropes of such stories: so, for example, it is rumoured that 'long ago one of [Bilbo's] Took ancestors must have taken a fairy wife', and Bilbo characterizes Gandalf as 'the fellow who used to tell such wonderful tales at parties, about dragons and goblins and giants and the rescue of princesses and the unexpected luck of widows' sons'. Smaug is said to 'carry away people, especially maidens, to eat', and when Bilbo sets out, he rides past 'old castles with an evil look, as if they had been built by wicked people'.

Unlike *The Lord of the Rings*, there are no dates in *The Hobbit*: the story is simply set 'long ago', Tolkien's equivalent of the fairy-tale opening, 'Once upon a time'.

Again unlike *The Lord of the Rings*, *The Hobbit* is full of episodes, individuals, and objects that remain unexplained, and this very lack of system is one of the pleasures the story gives: for the most part, it is simply one adventure after another, in the perilous world of 'Wilderland'. Most obviously, little history is supplied for Bilbo's ring. In the first edition of *The Hobbit*, it is simply a magic ring of invisibility, and Gollum renounces his claim to it when Bilbo wins the riddle contest.

The Lord of the Rings

The Lord of the Rings is set some decades after *The Hobbit*. Bilbo is now elderly, and has decided to pass his home and possessions over to his nephew Frodo. But Gandalf has discovered that the magic ring which Bilbo acquired on his earlier adventures is really the 'One Ring', an artefact of immense power forged in ages past by the Dark Lord Sauron, the lieutenant of Morgoth. Its reacquisition will enable Sauron to conquer and oppress the whole of Middle-earth (as Tolkien now calls the setting for his story), and his agents—so-called Black Riders, later revealed to be the undead Nazgûl—are now searching for it, and getting closer. So Frodo flees Hobbiton, accompanied by three hobbit friends: the well-to-do Merry and Pippin and his gardener-servant Sam. The ring can only be destroyed—and Sauron defeated—if it is cast into a fiery volcano, Mount Doom, in Sauron's own land of Mordor, and this is the quest which Frodo undertakes as 'ring-bearer', initially accompanied by a fellowship of travelling companions, including Gandalf the wizard, Aragorn a wandering ranger, the Elf Legolas, and the Dwarf Gimli.

The three volumes of *The Lord of the Rings* tell the stories of the four hobbits—sometimes together, sometimes separated—as they make their way through the tumultuous world events which Bilbo's possession of the ring has accidentally drawn them into. While the other members of the 'Fellowship of the Ring' find themselves engaged in battles, politics, and military service, the isolated Frodo and Sam creep closer and closer to Mount Doom and the climax of the story—a harrowing, burdensome journey far removed from the light-hearted adventures of Bilbo.

The Lord of the Rings delivers a thrilling, page-turning plot of great forward momentum—complex, exciting, and intricate—with the jeopardy at stake being nothing less than the fate of the free world, a fate that turns ultimately not on the clash of armies but rather the efforts of two little figures trudging into darkness. But the work offers its readers not only a narrative experience but also the discovery of a whole world. Here, the picaresque, one-thing-after-another adventures of *The Hobbit* are deepened and broadened into the creation of a series of peoples, places, and cultures for the reader to learn about, explore, and delight in: the ancient, sequestered Elves of Lothlórien, the slow-talking Ents of Fangorn Forest, the horse-warriors of Rohan, and so on. (We should note that from *The Lord of the Rings* onwards, Tolkien tended to capitalize the names of the different peoples of Middle-earth, such as Elves and Ents, and this practice is mostly followed here.) Tolkien's care and talents as a world-builder are supremely demonstrated in *The Lord of the Rings*: what the reader is being given is not just a story but a whole new world to inhabit and enjoy.

The Lord of the Rings is a vast and varied work, and we will explore many facets of this 'book of the century' in the chapters that follow. Unlike *The Hobbit*, with its obvious roots in fairy tales and children's literature, *The Lord of the Rings* fits into no recognizable genre of literature—or rather, it inadvertently created its own genre, later to be given the label of 'fantasy' (in some ways helpful, in others misleading). In the 1960s and 1970s, after the book's success, publishers sought frantically either to find the next

Tolkien or to reprint earlier works which might be marketed as proto-Tolkienian, but without any real success: there is nothing like *The Lord of the Rings*, though we will consider the question of sources in due course.

Part of the nature of this new type of writing, pioneered in *The Lord of the Rings*, was the combination of fairy tale and legend with modern realist fiction: while this story of half a million words is demonstrably a work of fiction written in the 1930s and 1940s—on Tolkien's part, a movement back towards the genre of the contemporary novel—at the same time it draws on all the elusive, enchanted qualities that Tolkien had earlier sought to capture in his 'Silmarillion' writings (and, to a lesser degree, in *The Hobbit*). This is the alchemy that Tolkien achieved, through skill and practice, as he treated the creatures and properties of fairy tales (and also medieval literature) in a pseudo-historical, narrative, world-building manner.

But even as it was one of Tolkien's great innovations, this combination of elements or genres—this movement from fairy tale to realist fiction—was also potentially one of his sources of difficulty, in that some features of the fairy-tale and legendary world proved more amenable to realist treatment than others. The Orcs, for example, have their origins in the goblins of fairy tales, and in the *Lost Tales* and *The Hobbit* they fulfil a narrative function as bogeys and enemies; no one weeps when their heads are chopped off by the protagonists. But a realist treatment is much more of a challenge, especially for a Christian such as Tolkien. Where did the Orcs come from? Could Morgoth or Sauron really have created them? Did they have free will or conscience? In his post-*Lord of the Rings* writings, Tolkien was to worry away at precisely these sorts of questions, provoked by the treatment of a fairy-tale world in a realist and morally serious manner.

The Lord of the Rings demonstrates Tolkien's system-making instincts much more fully than *The Hobbit*, from the Prologue

'Concerning Hobbits' through to the various appendices on history and language. And for quite a lot of the time, what he was trying to make cohere were his own earlier writings, both *The Hobbit* and the 'Silmarillion'. *The Hobbit* presented itself as a puzzle, almost as if it had been prepared by another hand, which Tolkien now had to rationalize, extend, and make consistent. Many unexplained elements in the earlier story were therefore given elaborate back stories, from Beorn, the Lonely Mountain, and the Necromancer, to Gollum, Gandalf, the Shire, and above all the Ring itself (which necessitated some rewriting of the relevant sections of *The Hobbit* for a revised edition). Meanwhile, in order to connect the 'Silmarillion' and *The Lord of the Rings*, Tolkien had to stitch together the two bodies of narrative into a single story-world—with the 'Second Age' legend of Númenor being one of the most important ways of doing this.

The Lord of the Rings was also revolutionary as a physical object, in terms of book history. It was written as one book, not three, but Tolkien's publishers (the relatively small firm of George Allen and Unwin) were unable to publish a book of such size as one volume; so they made the decision to publish the work as three volumes. Three-volume novels had been common in the second half of the 19th century (for example, George Eliot's *The Mill on the Floss*), but the twist here was that each volume of *The Lord of the Rings* was given its own title (rather than just being given a number), and the three volumes were published at staggered intervals (*The Fellowship of the Ring* in July 1954, *The Two Towers* in November 1954, and *The Return of the King* in October 1955). The result was not the resurgence of the Victorian 'triple-decker' novel but rather the new and unintended idea that the 'trilogy' should be the normal publishing format for fantasy fiction.

These three volumes also included maps, appendices, and even an index (planned for the first edition but only appearing in the second edition of 1966). A novel with maps and appendices is a strange and innovative idea, and all the obvious parallels are with works of non-fiction (such as travel books or translations of Icelandic sagas). The desirability of an index attests to the unparalleled nature of Tolkien's achievement as a world-builder and the appeal this made to his readership. A few other, pre-Tolkienian novels might have maps; but what other works of fiction have ever called for an index? There is—to repeat—nothing like *The Lord of the Rings*.

The 'Silmarillion' (2)

Tolkien finished writing *The Lord of the Rings* in 1948, though there was to be a good deal of revision before it was published in 1954–5. Its composition and completion, and the connecting of its contents with those of the 'Silmarillion' and *The Hobbit*, mark the point at which Tolkien's mythological and fictional writings, by now accumulated over thirty years, form a single coherent and consolidated 'legendarium'. It is no surprise, therefore, that Tolkien wished to see both the 'Silmarillion' and *The Lord of the Rings* published together, 'as one long Saga of the Jewels and the Rings', as he put it. In the event, this was not to be; but in the early 1950s, in the years between the drafting of *The Lord of the Rings* and its preparation for publication, Tolkien embarked on a wholesale overhaul of his 'Silmarillion' materials. These had been gathering dust through the decade-long writing of *The Lord of the Rings*, and Tolkien returned to the stories of the 'Silmarillion' with an astonishing energy and assurance—and now a hope, as well, of finding an audience for his mythology.

The major 'digest' works—the *Quenta Silmarillion* itself, and the bodies of annals—were revised, expanded, and reconsidered in countless ways, but with the usual Tolkienian tendency of failing to complete one round of revision before starting on another one elsewhere. Much of this was minor tinkering—changing names and genealogies, or refining plot motifs—but some was more fundamental. There were also lots of insertions to be made into the 'Silmarillion' of figures and features that had emerged in the writing of *The Lord of the Rings*, and sometimes these created knock-on effects: examples include Galadriel, the Ents, Moria, Arwen, and a greatly enhanced role for Sauron. The three 'great tales' were returned to as well, and each received a new version (again, incomplete). For Beren and Lúthien, the 1920s *Lay of Leithian* was recommenced, and a new prose version begun. For the Fall of Gondolin, there was an attempt at a new, full-length retelling (the first since the original version written in the First World War), but this did not extend far into the story. And for the tale of Túrin (or more correctly, the children of Húrin), Tolkien invested an enormous amount of time and effort in the 1950s in producing a major self-standing narrative (posthumously published, in edited form, both as *Narn i Hîn Húrin* in *Unfinished Tales* and as *The Children of Húrin* as an independent book). In these Túrin writings Tolkien was developing a new style of narrative, pitched midway between the archaic elevation of the *Quenta* and the novelistic storytelling of *The Lord of the Rings*.

In the later 1950s and 1960s, there were other new forms of writing too, of a less narrative and more philosophical, theological, or scientific nature. These examined questions such as reincarnation and remarriage among the Elves, the number of Elves that journeyed to Valinor, and the origin and agency of the Orcs. Such writings are often marked by a desire to specify, measure, and enumerate that is far from what we might think of as 'mythic' or 'mythopoeic' writing—they are subjecting the 'Silmarillion', as it were, to the same sort of treatment as the Third Age was given in the appendices to *The Lord of the Rings*. Such concerns also feature prominently in Tolkien's published *Letters*, most of which date from the 1950s and 1960s; but we should not generalize these preoccupations across his writing career, as we lack a comparable body of self-commentary from the 1920s and 1930s.

In these decades, Tolkien also sought to bring his invented world into a more direct compatibility with Christian belief. Most strikingly, in the text *Athrabeth Finrod ah Andreth*, a dialogue about mortality and immortality, a promise of the Incarnation is offered as the human wise woman Andreth speaks of what she calls 'the Old Hope' or 'the Great Hope', according to which 'the One will himself enter into Arda [i.e. the world], and heal Men and all the Marring from the beginning to the end'.

Some changes were made—or at least contemplated—for scientific reasons as well. Most fundamentally, in the original, pre-war versions of the 'Silmarillion', the Sun and the Moon are created only after Morgoth has destroyed the Two Trees of Valinor, as substitute (but lesser) sources of light. Now, however, Tolkien worried that such a plain contradiction of modern cosmology was problematic, and an alternative rationale for the myths—that the Elves' traditions were incorrect and unscientific—seemed intolerable to him, as it undermined the supreme status and wisdom of Elvish lore. So perhaps the Sun and Moon should be present from the creation? But then, if they were, that would diminish fatally the importance of the Silmarils, as the only surviving vessels of the light of the Two Trees... Tolkien seems to have hesitated, unsure of what to do.

How Tolkien intended—or hoped—to bring together a body of these 'Silmarillion' writings into a publishable volume or volumes remains unclear; and it is thanks to Christopher Tolkien's remarkable labours as executor and editor that we now have acquaintance with these evolving texts. There is something poignant, perhaps even heartbreaking, about some of these late writings, as we can observe the elderly Tolkien seeking to rationalize and explain the myths and presuppositions of the 'Silmarillion', and debating with himself whether to de-enchant his own mythology, thereby stripping it of the quality his younger self had valued so keenly—that of 'Faërie'.

Chapter 4
Faërie

'On Fairy-Stories'

When Bilbo approaches Rivendell for the first time in *The Hobbit*, he thinks excitedly, 'it smells like elves!' C. S. Lewis, reviewing the book on publication, picked out just this sentence and declared that 'it may be years before we produce another author with such a sharp nose for an elf'. Tolkien is, indisputably, the 20th century's greatest author of elves and the elvish, and this chapter explores the peculiar nature of the enchantment that he labelled 'Faërie'.

We can begin with theory, before turning to practice. Tolkien's essay 'On Fairy-Stories' was given as a lecture at the University of St Andrews in 1939 (in honour of the writer and folklorist Andrew Lang) and then published in extended form in 1947. In this major piece, he attempts to analyse what fairy tales are as a literary form, and what 'Faërie' is as a more abstract quality. The essay can be read as Tolkien's manifesto, or theorization, for the type of writing he was attempting in *The Lord of the Rings* (in progress in 1939, nearly finished in 1947), and it undoubtedly represents a series of reflections on his own art. But it is also a retrospective analysis of the previous sixty or seventy years of scholarship and composition in the field of fairy tales. Tolkien warns, however: 'Faërie cannot be caught in a net of words; for it is one of its qualities to be indescribable, though not imperceptible.'

Tolkien disputes that there is any inherent connection between fairy tales and children, and instead argues that what such stories have to offer to readers is 'Fantasy, Recovery, Escape, Consolation, all things of which children have, as a rule, less need than older people'. By 'Fantasy' Tolkien means both the bringing into being of imagined, secondary worlds (what he called 'sub-creation', explored also in his poem 'Mythopoeia') and also their attendant 'quality of strangeness and wonder'. 'Recovery' is the regaining of health and the refreshed ability to see each leaf, each flower, each object anew. 'Escape', not unrelated, is release from a narrow and prescribed diet of realist fiction, as well as from the alienating conditions of modern industrial society. And 'Consolation' represents the final, supreme quality that Tolkien believed fairy tales to offer: the promise of a happy ending. This is a fundamental notion, and something we will return to.

'On Fairy-Stories' supplies a rich exploration of its topic. One unexpected claim is Tolkien's belief that among the most profound human wishes satisfied by fairy tales is 'the desire to converse with other living things'—that is, with animals and other creatures. Talking animals are to be found frequently in Tolkien's own earlier works, from Tevildo, Prince of Cats, in *The Book of Lost Tales*, through children's stories such as *Roverandom*, and on to Roäc the raven in *The Hobbit*, before their prominence declines in *The Lord of the Rings* and later. Although the Ents might be regarded as a special case, we might not realize from his most famous work alone just how highly Tolkien valued this aspect of 'Faërie'.

Tolkien's essay amounts to a thorough—and, in time, a highly influential—championing of fairy tales and the art of 'sub-creation', as well as a blueprint for the writing of *The Lord of the Rings*. Some decades later, in his critical essay on *Smith of Wootton Major*, he wrote with equal earnestness that 'the love of Faery is the love of love: a relationship towards all things, animate and inanimate, which includes love and respect, and removes or modifies the spirit of possession and domination'; therefore, he concludes, "Faery' is as necessary for the health and complete functioning of the Human as is sunlight for physical life'. Did Tolkien actually believe in fairies and the like, one might wonder? He seems always to choose his words carefully on this issue, and never committed himself to a statement that such beings were purely fictional or imaginary.

Mortals in Fairyland

In 'On Fairy-Stories', Tolkien insists that 'stories that are actually concerned primarily with 'fairies', that is with creatures that might also in modern English be called 'elves', are relatively rare and as a rule not very interesting', and that instead 'most good 'fairy-stories' are about the *aventures* of men in the Perilous Realm or upon its shadowy marches'. In his writings, he repeatedly stages precisely this sort of encounter, well attested in earlier folktales and medieval literature, between mortals and elves; and he was fascinated by what the Anglo-Saxon personal name Ælfwine, 'elf-friend', might have betokened.

The frame narrative of *The Book of Lost Tales* sees a human traveller (first called Eriol, later Ælfwine) reaching Tol Eressëa, the Lonely Isle of the Elves, and there learning their lore. Moreover, all three of the 'great tales' in the collection follow this pattern, being focalized through a male, human protagonist who meets Elves: Beren falls in love with the elf-maiden Lúthien, Túrin comes to the kingdoms of Doriath and Nargothrond, and Tuor finds the great city of Gondolin.

This mortal desire to encounter fairies or elves is present from Tolkien's first public piece of 'Faërie' writing, the poem 'Goblin Feet' (published in 1915). The narrator of this slight piece expresses a desire to 'follow in [the] train' of a band of fairies or gnomes, and feels a keen yearning for these otherworldly creatures ('O! it's knocking at my heart— | Let me go! O! let me start!') and a poignant 'sorrow' when they have gone. When

Tolkien unsuccessfully submitted a collection of his early poetry to a publisher in 1916, the volume was titled *The Trumpets of Fairie*.

Tolkien's early Elves often have 'elfin' or 'fairy' qualities about them, not only in poems such as 'Goblin Feet' but also in *The Book of Lost Tales* and beyond. In *The Hobbit*, Bilbo and the dwarves have a fruitless time trying to reach the campfires of the merry, singing Elves of Mirkwood; and for many years, including in the first edition of *The Hobbit*, Tolkien designated the Noldoli or Noldor, the leading Elves of his mythology, as 'Gnomes' (as in the 1930 *Quenta Noldorinwa*, which is subtitled 'the brief History of the Noldoli or Gnomes'). In due course the quality of levity or prettiness was reduced or removed: Tolkien rejected the adjective 'elfin' for the later, preferred form 'elven', and he also abandoned the designation of 'Gnomes' (though it survives as a kind of linguistic joke in *The Silmarillion*, where the narrator states that 'Men called King Felagund, whom they first met of all the Eldar [i.e. High Elves], Nóm, that is Wisdom, in the language of that people'). A renewed emphasis was given to the stature and dignity of the Elves, and the playful people of *The Hobbit*, as found in Rivendell and Mirkwood, are upgraded to a more decorous seriousness in *The Lord of the Rings*. But the guiding notion of mortals in Fairyland endured. *The Adventures of Tom Bombadil* (1962) ends with the poem 'The Last Ship', in which a mortal woman yearns to leave with the Elves, and it is also at the heart of *Smith of Wootton Major* (1967), Tolkien's last published story in his lifetime.

In *The Lord of the Rings*, to enter the forest-enclave of Lothlórien is to enter Faërie. The suspicious Boromir describes Lothlórien as a 'perilous land', a judgement modified by Aragorn to 'fair and perilous'. When Frodo's eyes are uncovered there, it seems to him that he has stepped into 'a vanished world' and that 'a light was upon it for which his language had no name'. His senses experience just the kind of recovery that Tolkien had adumbrated in 'On Fairy-Stories': 'he saw no colour but those he knew, gold and white and blue and green, but they were fresh and poignant, as if he had at that moment first perceived them'. When he touches the trunk of a tree, 'never before had he been so suddenly and so keenly aware of the feel and texture of a tree's skin and of the life within it'. His companion Sam exclaims of Lothlórien that 'this is more Elvish than anything I ever heard tell of', as if he was *inside* a song'. Aragorn concurs: 'Here is the heart of Elvendom on earth.'

The notion that time in Fairyland moves differently is an old one. While in Lothlórien, Frodo feels as if he is 'in a timeless land that did not fade or change', and as the Fellowship depart, they realize that 'they could not count the days and nights that they had passed there'. Sam perceives that 'magic' is a misleading word for the type of enchantment that lies upon Faërie: 'If there's any magic about, it's right down deep, where I can't lay my hands on it.'

Elves are at the centre of Tolkien's mythology, which is thus not anthropocentric. Tolkien's Elves are artists, surpassingly skilful in their crafts and making; they are inhabitants of the natural world, in harmony with the living earth and its creatures and materials; they are wise and filled with memory and learning; and they are touched by sorrow and exile. But they are often viewed from the outside, by the mortals who come into contact with them and fall under their enchantment.

Dwindling and departing

Tolkien's Elves are also immortal, though they can be killed by weapons. They thus have a profoundly different relationship with time than do mortal humans. In his late, post-*Lord of the Rings* essays, Tolkien theorized that the Elves were in fact 'coeval' with the Earth, and thus not actually timeless—although they might well seem so to short-lived mortals. Indeed, he argued that the Elves 'did not (and do not) *live* slowly', but rather 'they move and think swifter than Men, and achieve more than any Man in any given length of time'.

Nonetheless, a central fact about the Elves, from the beginning to the end of Tolkien's writing career, is that in some way they will fade or disappear, to be superseded eventually by Men. The last sections of *The Book of Lost Tales* were never written, but Tolkien's notes tell us that, in one scheme for its conclusion, 'great ages elapse; Men spread and thrive, and the Elves of the Great Lands fade'. In these early ideas, Tolkien also speculated that the Elves experienced a gradual reduction in stature ('as Men wax more powerful and numerous so the fairies fade and grow small and tenuous, filmy and transparent [...] At last Men, or almost all, can no longer see the fairies'), thus bridging the gap between the grand and martial Elves of the *Lost Tales* and Victorian and Edwardian conventions. The last paragraph of the *Quenta Noldorinwa* (1930), somewhat differently, records of the work's contents that 'some of these things are sung and said yet by the fading Elves; and more still are sung by the vanished Elves that dwell now on the Lonely Isle'.

The idea that elves and fairies had vanished from the world was not unique to Tolkien but rather a commonplace of contemporary 'Faërie' writing. The fairies, it was held, had been driven out by industrialization, or urbanization, or secularization. In Rudyard Kipling's *Puck of Pook's Hill* (1906), the fairies leave England en masse at the time of the Reformation; and the furore over the so-called Cottingley Fairies in 1920 points to an urgent, contested desire to rediscover the fairy world (the title of Arthur Conan Doyle's 1922 book on the subject, *The Coming of the Fairies*, sounds as if it could be of one of Tolkien's *Lost Tales*).

The departure of the Elves continues to be a recurrent note in *The Lord of the Rings*, giving a mournful mood of elegiac ending. But now the explanation for this has changed, and the Elves are departing Middle-earth to return home to the Undying Lands in the west. Lothlórien is again the crucial setting, where Galadriel explains to Frodo that the defeat of Sauron will usher in the dominion of Men and thereby seal the decline of the Elves: 'If you succeed, then our power is diminished, and Lothlórien will fade, and the tides of Time will sweep it away. We must depart into the West, or dwindle to a rustic folk of dell and cave, slowly to forget and to be forgotten.' The familiar vocabulary is here: 'diminish', 'fade', 'depart', 'dwindle'. In the epilogue which Tolkien wrote for *The Lord of the Rings* (but in the end decided not to publish), we see Sam, now older, talking to his children. His daughters Elanor and Rose want to see Elves, just as he did when he was young: "But the Elves are sailing away still, aren't they, and soon there'll be none, will there, dad?' said Rose; 'and then all will be just places, and very nice, but, but..." In reply, Sam tells them that 'Elves are sad; and that's what makes them so beautiful'.

Once again, in his post-*Lord of the Rings* reconsiderations, Tolkien explored a number of theological or metaphysical reasons for the vanishing of the Elves. Even though the departure of the Elves west-over-sea was now a fixed narrative point, Tolkien never quite abandoned his earlier, alternative notion that the Elves were fading as well as departing. In the treatise *Laws and Customs among the Eldar*, the Elvish opinion is recorded that, as their spirits consume their bodies over time, before the world ends 'all the Eldalië on earth will have become as spirits invisible to mortal eyes'. The dialogue text *Athrabeth Finrod ah Andreth* states of the Elves that '[they] find their supersession by Men a mystery, and a cause of grief'.

As we have seen, the reflections of the elderly Tolkien sometimes serve to de-enchant the 'Silmarillion', and the continued emphasis on the disappearance of the Elves may have something to do with Tolkien's own processes of ageing. But the idea of diminishment and departure is there from the beginning, and Tolkien's treatment of this idea represents his own elegiac twist to a wider cultural trope.

Elves and England

In a letter to the publisher Milton Waldman, probably in 1951, Tolkien wrote:

> Once upon a time (my crest has long since fallen) I had a mind to make a body of more or less connected legend, ranging from the large and cosmogonic, to the level of romantic fairy-story — the larger founded on the lesser in contact with the earth, the lesser drawing splendour from the vast backcloths — which I could dedicate simply to: to England; to my country.

This letter is often paraphrased as indicating Tolkien's desire to create (in a commonly used phrase) a 'mythology for England', and it is sometimes deployed as a gloss to *The Lord of the Rings* among other works. But we should note that that is not what Tolkien actually says here (indeed, he never used the phrase 'mythology for England', which comes instead from his biographer, Humphrey Carpenter), and it is clear from this 1951 letter that he is writing of an ambition that is now long in the past. In other words, this letter is not talking about *The Lord of the Rings* but rather *The Book of Lost Tales*.

The *Lost Tales*, and associated poems, imagine the Lonely Isle of Tol Eressëa as being physically the same land as England (or perhaps the island of Britain). Places in modern England are equated with Elvish places in Tol Eressëa: for example, the town of Warwick is the Elvish Kortirion and the county of Warwickshire is Alalminórë, while the village of Great Haywood in Staffordshire is Tavrobel, to which Eriol comes (Warwick and Great Haywood were important places to Tolkien, where his wife Edith had lived). The implication is that England is an enchanted place, the home (or at least once the home) of Elves: the 1915 poem 'Kortirion among the Trees' presents Warwick as 'the inmost province of the fading isle | Where linger yet the Lonely Companies'—that is to say, 'The holy fairies and immortal elves | That dance among the trees and sing themselves | A wistful song of things that were, and could be yet'.

This collocation of elves and England was not unusual in the Edwardian period. In Charles M. Doughty's patriotic verse drama *The Cliffs* (1909), for example, a community of elves are among those who are guarding England from invasion. More significantly, Kipling's *Puck of Pook's Hill*—a work which influenced Tolkien in a number of ways—presents England as being 'not any common Earth, | Water or wood or air', but rather 'Merlin's Isle of Gramarye', an enchanted place marked by the presence of the many 'Old Things' who once lived there, prior to their eventual departure over sea. As Puck says: 'I saw them come into Old England and I saw them go. Giants, trolls, kelpies, brownies, goblins, imps; wood, tree, mound, and water spirits; heath-people, hill-watchers, treasure-guards, good people, little people, pishogues, leprechauns, night-riders, pixies, nixies, gnomes, and the rest—gone, all gone!'

The nature of the connection between England and his mythology shifted as Tolkien worked on the 'Silmarillion' through the 1920s and 1930s. In the original, Eriol-stage of the *Lost Tales*, the island of Tol Eressëa becomes England (or Britain) through the passing of time and the settlement of humans. Later, the two islands became separate places, but England still retains its Elvish heritage as a surviving fragment of the lands of Beleriand, shattered at the end of the wars with Morgoth (in an annotation to the *Quenta Noldorinwa*, an alternative name of Beleriand is said to be 'Ingolondë the fair and sorrowful'). Later still, during the process of writing *The Lord of the Rings* and making it fit with the 'Silmarillion', this idea too seems to have been abandoned, so that England was no longer to be regarded as a special place due to its historical connection to the Elves, except perhaps through the transmission of their legends. Was this also a sign of Tolkien's loss of enchantment in middle and old age? Maybe so. But there may be another answer too, which is that, in *The Lord of the Rings*, Englishness gets relocated from a place to a people.

Hobbits

The word *hobbit* was added to the *Oxford English Dictionary* in 1976 and defined as follows: 'In the tales of J. R. R. Tolkien (1892–1973): one of an imaginary people, a small variety of the human race, that gave themselves this name (meaning 'hole-dweller') but were called by others halflings, since they were half the height of normal men.' The entry was published by Robert Burchfield, Tolkien's former doctoral student, but was based on a draft prepared by Tolkien himself in his lifetime. The word *hobbit* does in fact occur in a source earlier than Tolkien's own writings—the so-called *Denham Tracts*, a collection of mid-Victorian folklore—where it features among a vast list of miscellaneous folkloric and supernatural beings (the relevant section goes, 'dudmen, hell-hounds, dopple-gangers, boggleboes, bogies, redmen, portunes, grants, hobbits, hobgoblins, brown-men, cowies, dunnies, wirrikows'). But whether or not Tolkien knew of this earlier source—and the evidence is debatable—the question arises as to whether his hobbits should or should not be counted among the inhabitants of Faërie. How elfin or otherwise are these peaceable, gregarious hole-dwellers? The *Oxford English Dictionary* entry views them as being at the same time both 'imaginary' and also related to 'normal men'.

The opening of *The Hobbit* invites us to view hobbits as falling among the inhabitants of Faërie, albeit with some qualifications. 'I suppose hobbits need some description nowadays', the narrator says, 'since they have become rare and shy of the Big People, as they call us.' This aligns hobbits with the vanishing fairies of the late 19th and early 20th centuries, and also with folkloric beings such as hobs and brownies. The narrator continues, however: 'There is little or no magic about them, except the ordinary everyday sort which helps them to disappear quietly and quickly

46

when large stupid folk like you and me come blundering along.' The implication is that some hobbits are still out there, as shy and retiring creatures in the modern world.

The scholarly narrator of the Prologue to *The Lord of the Rings* still speaks of them in the present tense: 'Hobbits are an unobtrusive but very ancient people, more numerous formerly than they are today […] they love peace and quiet and good tilled earth […] Even in ancient days they were, as a rule, shy of 'the Big Folk', as they call us, and now they avoid us with dismay and are becoming hard to find.' *The Lord of the Rings* represents a massive expansion in hobbit-lore: in accordance with Tolkien's characteristic processes, the world of the hobbits has now become systematized and historicized, with a well-developed culture able to be treated anthropologically. The Prologue alone tells us of their history, geography, clothing, architecture, love of 'pipeweed', and system of government. *The Fellowship of the Ring* also presents us with a map of the Shire (as their home is now called). Everything is more detailed, more calendared, and more explicit. But the sense of hobbits as being, in human eyes, mysterious or even mythical creatures persists within *The Lord of the Rings* itself: in Rohan, hobbits are held to be 'only a little people in old songs and children's tales' and a 'folk of legend', while in the city of Minas Tirith, Faramir (who has earlier encountered Frodo and Sam) tells Pippin that he is 'not the first halfling that I have seen walking out of northern legends into the Southlands'.

The Lord of the Rings also develops the implied association between hobbits and England. The hobbits of the Shire represent a type of Englishness, close to Tolkien's heart, that is at once both prosaic and mythical. The two founding brothers, Marcho and Blanco, who migrate west over the River Baranduin, are transparently modelled on Hengest and Horsa, legendary founders of Anglo-Saxon England (all four names mean 'horse' in some way), and the three hobbit tribes of Stoors, Harfoots, and Fallohides parallel the Angles, Saxons, and Jutes. The place-names of the Shire are redolent of those of such counties as Oxfordshire and Berkshire—dominantly Old English, but with a Celtic component. Pre-industrial life in Hobbiton is an idealized image of the Victorian village community. The blend of warmth and formality, the respect for time-honoured customs, and the suspicion of grand narratives, all speak to a certain English self-image or self-myth. Hobbits are often insular and unadventurous. 'You should never have gone mixing yourself up with Hobbiton folk, Mr Frodo,' Farmer Maggot says, showing how one part of the Shire looks askance at another. When Gaffer Gamgee relates his encounter with a Black Rider, he reports that 'He spoke funny'.

But hobbits are also resourceful and enduring, inviting certain parallels with English self-conceptions from the time of the Second World War. 'Ease and peace', the Prologue tells us, 'had left this people still curiously tough': they are described as being 'difficult to daunt' and 'doughty at bay', and they could 'survive rough handling [...] in a way that astonished those who did not know them well and looked no further than their bellies and their well-fed faces'. These qualities are seen supremely in Frodo and Sam's journey into Mordor, but they are also evidenced by the adventures of Merry and Pippin in Rohan and Gondor: after the latter pair's escape from the elite Orcs of the Uruk-hai, the narrator reports that 'no listener would have guessed from their words that they had suffered cruelly, and been in dire peril', and at the Battle of the Pelennor Fields, Merry finds that 'suddenly the slow-kindled courage of his race awoke', so fulfilling Elrond's earlier prediction that 'this is the hour of the Shire-folk'.

Tolkien stated that Hobbiton was intended to be 'at about the latitude of Oxford'. Hobbits therefore stand in many ways in a relationship to the early- and mid-20th-century idea of the 'Little Englander': home-loving patriots, with little interest in the world beyond, and a set of traits that might seem quaint and even parochial—but who are not to be underestimated or pushed around. Hobbits, we can say, face two ways, as both inhabitants of Faërie and also transpositions of a certain idea of Englishness into the archaic world of Middle-earth.

Chapter 5
Language

Linguistic aesthetics

Tolkien's Elves are artists and creators, and this is especially true in terms of language. Of the Noldor in Valinor, Tolkien wrote in the later *Quenta Silmarillion* that 'Great became their knowledge and their skill; yet even greater was their thirst for more knowledge [...] They were changeful in speech, for they had great love of words, and sought ever to find names more fit for all things that they knew or imagined.' Furthermore, in the treatise *Laws and Customs among the Eldar*, Tolkien explained that 'the Noldor were of all the Eldar the swiftest in acquiring word-mastery', and revealed that the Noldor even had a special word, *lámatyávë*, meaning 'individual pleasure in the sounds and forms of words'. What is more, among the Noldor, 'this *lámatyávë* was held a mark of individuality, and more important indeed than others, such as stature, colour, and features of face'. Elsewhere, in a long essay called *Quendi and Eldar*, Tolkien explained that the eminence of the Noldor as linguists was 'shown not so much in the acquisition of new tongues as in their love of language, their inventiveness, and their concern with the lore of language, and the history and relations of different tongues. In adopting a word for use in their own tongue (which they loved) Elves fitted it to their own style for aesthetic reasons.'

Tolkien's Elves, in other words, are aesthetic philologists—just like Tolkien himself. The commitment to *lámatyávë*, to 'pleasure in the sounds and forms of words', was a guiding principle in Tolkien's linguistic and literary art, and he claimed that the aesthetics of the names in *The Lord of the Rings* had 'given perhaps more pleasure to more readers than anything else in it'. That such a thing as 'linguistic aesthetics' exist, and that they are of profound importance, was one of Tolkien's strongest and most distinctive beliefs.

This belief is expressed most fully in his essay 'English and Welsh' (delivered as a lecture in 1955 and published in 1963). There, Tolkien asserts that 'most English-speaking people, for instance, will admit that *cellar door* is 'beautiful', especially if dissociated from its sense (and from its spelling). More beautiful than, say, *sky*, and far more beautiful than *beautiful*.' For him personally, in the Welsh language '*cellar doors* are extraordinarily frequent'—that is to say, the sounds and combinations of the language gave him repeated pleasure. He acknowledges that 'the nature of this *pleasure* is difficult, perhaps impossible, to analyse', though the process of linguistic analysis may help to '[make] more precise some of the features of style that are pleasing or distasteful'. Tolkien suggested that the accessing and awareness of such pleasure might be 'felt most strongly in the study of a 'foreign' or second-learned language', and in an earlier essay he proposed that the 'compensation' one receives in the study of a dead language is 'a great freshness of perception of the word-form'.

This earlier essay, 'A Secret Vice', explores the pleasures of invented—and of inventing—languages. In creating his own languages, Tolkien explained that he was 'personally most interested perhaps in word-form in itself, and in word-form in relation to meaning (so-called phonetic fitness) than in any other department'. Both of Tolkien's two main Elvish languages, Quenya and Sindarin (earlier called Noldorin, and earlier still Goldogrin), were consciously modelled on real-world languages that held a deep aesthetic appeal for him: Quenya on Finnish and Sindarin on Welsh. A character in his unfinished novel *The Notion Club Papers*, Arundel Lowdham, confesses his teenage enthusiasm for Anglo-Saxon or Old English: 'I liked its word-style, I think. It wasn't so much what was written in it as the flavour of the words that suited me.' When Lowdham then encounters Quenya, he finds it 'beautiful, in its simple and euphonious style'. Tolkien himself wondered if Finnish, the inspiration for Quenya, might even suffer from 'an excess of euphony'.

If, according to Tolkien, some languages or forms might be perceived (subjectively) as beautiful, this must also imply that some other languages or forms might be regarded as ugly or possessed of some other associational value. In *The Hobbit*, we are told of 'the dreadful language of the Wargs': Bilbo cannot understand it, but 'it sounded terrible to him, as if all their talk was about cruel and wicked things, as it was'. In *The Lord of the Rings*, Gandalf describes the language of Orcs as 'hideous', and the narrator refers to 'their abominable tongue'; a snippet of orc-speech is given as '*Uglúk u bagronk sha pushdug Saruman-glob búbhosh skai*'.

In *The Notion Club Papers*, Lowdham suggests that it is in the relation of word-form to meaning that the artistry of language-making resides: 'it is difficult to fit meaning to any given sound-pattern', he states, 'and even more difficult to fit a sound-pattern to any given meaning'. But this is the skill that may be acclaimed as 'language-building' rather than mere 'code-making'. As soon becomes obvious to readers of *The Lord of the Rings*, the names of persons and places in the story are not meaningless sequences of sound: most names have semantically appropriate meanings too. However, Tolkien does not normally supply name-etymologies within the text, though dedicated readers can no doubt work out some of the semantics and grammar—for example, that *dor* means 'land' or 'country' (Mordor, Gondor,

Eriador), that *amon* means 'hill' and its plural is the mutated *emyn* (Amon Hen, Emyn Muil), and that the suffix *-rim* indicates a group plural (Galadhrim, Haradrim, Rohirrim).

As in the real world, it makes sense for place-names to have semantically appropriate meanings: Mordor is 'dark-land', Gondor 'stone-land', and so on. This is odder for personal names, though. It is not a problem that, say, the two sons of the half-elven Elrond should be called Elrohir and Elladan (Tolkien suggested 'Elf-knight' and 'Elf-Númenórean' as translations), but what about Celeborn 'silver-tall', for example, or (from the 'Silmarillion') Maeglin 'sharp glance'? How could a person's mature appearance or character have been known at the time of their birth and name-giving? Conscious of this problem, and as part of his process of rationalization, Tolkien later posited elaborate processes of name-acquisition among the Elves: these included the giving of 'names of insight' or of 'foresight', when a mother 'might give a name to her child, indicating some dominant feature of its nature as perceived by her, or some foresight of its special fate', and also a self-determined ceremony, undertaken at a later stage in life, called the *Essecilmë* or 'Name-choosing'. The name Maeglin, Tolkien wrote, was only given to its bearer 'in boyhood, when these characteristics were recognized', while the name of Eärendil or Earendel, the great mariner, was glossed as 'sea-lover' and held to be 'prophetic'.

The philology of Elvish

So the names and words we encounter in *The Lord of the Rings* and Tolkien's other works are not arbitrary strings of sounds, and nor are they simply well-patterned sequences with distinctive linguistic flavours: instead, they are samples of a complex system of language, with each name or word having its own consistent form, meaning, and grammar. But even that is not all, remarkable enough though that is. Tolkien was a philologist, and his Elvish languages are invented and represented according to the key tenets of 19th- and early 20th-century philology. This means that Tolkien's languages are treated both historically and comparatively, with exceptionally detailed linguistic histories. It is this dimension that sets Tolkien's achievement apart from that of other makers of constructed languages (which tend to have grammar and vocabulary but not history).

As with nearly all other aspects of his 'Silmarillion' mythology, Tolkien's Elvish languages underwent repeated revisions across the course of his writing career (for example, it was only the publication of *The Lord of the Rings* that fixed the name of one of his two main languages as Sindarin as opposed to Noldorin, which is what it had been called for the preceding three decades). But a text from the mid-1930s, the *Lhammas* or 'Account of Tongues', gives us a good sense of the principles and complexities of the linguistic history of Elvish after some twenty years of work. This explains that the Elves learned language from the Valar themselves (an idea Tolkien later rejected), but Elvish began to diverge from 'Valarin' almost immediately, as the Elves were susceptible to the movement of time, unlike the Valar, and because 'Elves love the making of words, and this has ever been the chief cause of the change and variety of their tongues' (indicating that for Tolkien, linguistic change might occur for conscious, deliberate reasons, at least among Elves, and was not solely an unconscious or impersonal process). Separation and contact led to various subtypes of Elvish, most importantly Quenya and Noldorin/ Sindarin. Quenya was the older and more elevated of the two, a sort of 'Elf-latin' (as Tolkien called it) which arose among the Elves in Valinor and which 'became early fixed [...] as a language of high speech and of writing, and as a common speech among all Elves'. Noldorin/Sindarin, on the other hand, diverged from Quenya through processes of geographical separation and change over time, especially in Middle-earth as opposed to Aman, where, as the *Lhammas* explains, 'growth and change were swift for all living things'. Tolkien repeatedly reconsidered the relationship between Quenya and Noldorin/Sindarin and the reasons for their difference, and in the published *Silmarillion*, a more efficient explanation is given: Sindarin was the language of those Elves who never went to Valinor, which those who returned also adopted.

But this is just the external history of Tolkien's two Elvish languages, and excludes many shades of dialectal difference, as represented in the linguistic family trees that accompany the *Lhammas*. This external history was fully realized in the internal structures of the languages; and the posthumous publication of Tolkien's language papers (mostly in the specialist journals *Vinyar Tengwar* and *Parma Eldalamberon*) has revealed the astounding detail in which he developed Quenya and Noldorin/Sindarin, as he compiled lengthy historical grammars of their phonology and morphology.

This is where the comparative dimension of Tolkien's philological approach comes in. For Quenya and Noldorin/Sindarin, although modelled on two real-life languages that are wholly unrelated (Welsh is an Indo-European language but Finnish is not), are in Tolkien's linguistic history both derived from the same parent language, Common Eldarin (itself derived from Primitive Quendian). To devise and map their correspondences and divergences is an astonishing labour of reconstruction and explains why Tolkien, in terms of the basic building blocks of his Elvish vocabularies, proceeded not from the word but rather the 'root' (a fundamental concept for 19th-century philology). The *Etymologies*, a work mostly of the late 1930s, sets out these roots in alphabetical order: AM-, for example, means 'up', and leads to such words as Quenya *amba* 'upwards' and Noldorin/Sindarin *amon* 'hill'; or NAR- means 'flame, fire', and leads to Quenya *narqelion* 'fire-fading, autumn' and Noldorin/Sindarin *naur* 'flame' (as in the Sammath Naur in *The Lord of the Rings*). Quenya and Noldorin/Sindarin are related to one another according to a set of complex and systematic sound-changes: Eldarin KW-, for example, develops into Quenya *q(u)* but Noldorin/Sindarin *p* (compare Quenya *q(u)enta* 'tale' with the Noldorin/Sindarin *pennas* 'history', both derived from KWET- 'say'), or Eldarin TH- becomes *s* in Quenya but remains *th* in Noldorin/Sindarin (compare *soron* with *thoron*, both meaning 'eagle').

The posthumous publication of Tolkien's linguistic papers has demonstrated that the samples of Elvish in *The Lord of the Rings* really were only the tiniest tip of an enormous iceberg of language invention. Tolkien was insistent that the languages had come first, and that his mythology had been created to supply a history for those languages and their speakers, not the other way round: the first invention of Tolkien's two Elvish languages preceded the composition of *The Book of Lost Tales*. The languages and names never stood still, but over more than fifty years they were continuously revised and refined both in structure and meaning.

Notwithstanding the *Etymologies*, and also two early dictionaries of the languages, it is important to realize that the vocabulary and syntax of Tolkien's Elvish tongues remained less fully developed than their phonology and morphology; this too was in keeping with the emphases of academic philology. This means that, perhaps unexpectedly, Tolkien did not actually write extensive texts in his invented languages: in fact, he told an acquaintance on one occasion that he 'would indeed do a story in Elvish if only he knew enough Elvish'. In this respect, in spite of the decades of labour, Quenya and Noldorin/Sindarin do not resemble other invented languages such as Esperanto (of which Tolkien was an ardent supporter) which did produce lengthy works. (The inclusion of speeches in Elvish in modern adaptations of Tolkien's works have required the creation of what has been dubbed 'Neo-Elvish', attempting to fill in the gaps.) When Tolkien translated his own works into another language at any length, what he fabricated were Old English versions, not the original Elvish texts from which the Old English versions were supposedly derived. Tolkien's own writings in Elvish tend to be quite short, and he directed his efforts more to the creation of poetry (complete with Elvish verse-forms) than long speeches or prose works. In Tolkien's own lifetime, the most extensive Elvish text which he published was a poem, Galadriel's lament *Namárië* in *The Lord of the Rings*, for which later, in 1968, he supplied a linguistic gloss in the song-cycle *The Road Goes Ever On* with Donald Swann. The posthumous publication of many of Tolkien's linguistic writings has revealed many pleasures, such as the translation of the Lord's Prayer into both Quenya and Sindarin ('Ae Adar nín i vi Menel'), but no extensive narrative texts.

A multilingual world

Tolkien had been working on Quenya and Noldorin/Sindarin for over two decades by the time he started to write *The Lord of the Rings*. The composition of that work, with its great elaboration of the 'Third Age' of Middle-earth, led to the development or invention of a number of other languages, including Dwarvish or Khuzdul, Entish, and the 'Black Speech' of Mordor. Meanwhile, *The Notion Club Papers*, written during a pause on the greater work, produced extensive material on Adûnaic, the language of Númenor. As with the more extensive Elvish languages, these new tongues were developed mostly with respect to their phonology and morphology rather than vocabulary or syntax; but even within these limitations, the extent and care of Tolkien's labour was remarkable. These languages all had different flavours or linguistic aesthetics: no reader could confuse Dwarvish place-names such as Kheled-zâram and Zirakzigil with the agglutinative structures of Entish ('*a-lalla-lalla-rumba-kamanda-lind-or-burúmë*'). Tolkien also devised the notion of 'Westron' or 'Common Speech', a shared language of communication in Middle-earth that derived from the Adûnaic brought by Númenórean exiles.

Middle-earth is thus a multilingual world. It is also a world in which Tolkien gives us a great deal of linguistic information which might be better characterized as sociolinguistic rather than philological. Notwithstanding the narrative function of Westron to permit unmarked or everyday communication, Tolkien's stories are filled with moments of bilingualism, translation, language contact, and diglossia (that is, language-switching according to context)—in addition to discourses on linguistic history. This is present from the start, in the *Lost Tales*, but the multilingualism of Middle-earth is vastly enhanced and foregrounded in *The Lord of the Rings*.

So, for example, when Pippin is captured by Orcs at the start of *The Two Towers*, he finds to his surprise that 'much of the talk was intelligible; many of the Orcs were using ordinary language', and the reason given is that 'apparently the members of two or three quite different tribes were present, and they could not understand one another's orc-speech'. Later, Merry experiences the same 'surprise' when the wild man Ghân-buri-Ghân of Drúadan Forest 'spoke the Common Speech, though in a halting fashion'. Haldir the Elf, welcoming the Fellowship to Lothlórien, uses 'the Common Language, speaking slowly'. When Aragorn, Legolas, and Gimli are in pursuit of the captured hobbits, the Elf 'sing[s] softly to himself in his own tongue', but clearly uses the Common Speech to communicate with his two companions. When they meet the Riders of Rohan, the latter greet them 'using the Common Speech of the West'.

Various forms of individual or societal bilingualism are the norm in Middle-earth (which suggests that the contented monolingualism of hobbits may be yet another reflex of the Shire as England). The Ents are bilingual or multilingual. They speak Elvish but with a syntax influenced by Entish, so that Merry and Pippin are unsure whether Treebeard is 'humming in Entish or Elvish or some strange tongue' (most of the recorded examples of Entish language are described by Tolkien as 'fragments of Elf-speech strung together in Ent-fashion'). Haldir the Elf is able to speak the Common Speech because he has 'go[ne] abroad for the gathering of news', whereas his brothers, remaining in Lothlórien, 'speak little' of Westron. The Gondorians whom Frodo and Sam encounter in Ithilien speak first the Common Speech and then Elvish, and the minstrel at the Field of Cormallen sings 'now in the elven-tongue, now in the speech of the West'. Bilingual inscriptions in Middle-earth include Balin's tomb in Moria, 'written in the tongues of Men and Dwarves', and the memorial stone for Snowmane the horse, which is 'carved in the tongues of Gondor and the Mark'.

But although Westron is the Common Speech of Middle-earth, it is the Elvish languages that remain at the apex of Tolkien's multilingual culture. At the climax of *The Two Towers*, in a moment of great jeopardy, Frodo cries out in Quenya '*Aiya Eärendil Elenion Ancalima!*' and 'knew not what he had spoken'; shortly afterwards, Elvish words (in Sindarin) come also to Sam, as 'his tongue was loosed and his voice cried in a language which he did not know', in the invocation '*A Elbereth Gilthoniel*'. Here, the gifting to individuals of an unknown language in time of peril seems to signal the Elvish tongues as possessing a kind of specialness or even sanctity which the other languages of Middle-earth cannot aspire to.

Transmission and translation

The Hobbit tells us that Bilbo 'liked runes and letters and cunning handwriting', and the *Quenta Silmarillion* records that it was in Valinor that 'the Noldor first bethought them of letters, and Rúmil of Tirion was the name of the loremaster who first achieved fitting signs for the recording of speech and song'. Once again, *The Hobbit* offers us an exuberant act of inspiration, with the co-option of Anglo-Saxon runes for use on Thror's Map, while *The Lord of the Rings* detaches the runes from their real-world origins and supplies a secondary-world systematization: the appendices to *The Lord of the Rings* give analyses of the two main scripts to be found in Middle-earth, namely the cursive *tengwar* and the runic *cirth*. (Elvish *tengwar* can be found fleetingly in *The Hobbit*, written on the great jars in the illustration 'Conversation with

Smaug'.) Tolkien wrote English texts in *tengwar* to produce ornate display-pages of his private writings, and both runes and *tengwar* featured on the title-pages of *The Lord of the Rings* as first published.

This emphasis on the act of writing connects to Tolkien's preoccupation with questions of transmission. This goes back to the very beginnings of his mythology. *The Book of Lost Tales* was conceived as being a collection of stories which the wanderer Eriol learned from the Elves of Tol Eressëa and brought back to his own land. This idea continued after the figure of Eriol was replaced by the Anglo-Saxon seafarer Ælfwine, and the notion that knowledge of the 'Silmarillion' stories was transmitted via Ælfwine then remained a core element in Tolkien's conceptualization of his mythology over several decades: many texts are presented as being his translations, supposedly based on works or information supplied by the Elvish scholar Pengolod or Pengolodh. But in the end, the longstanding and pivotal figure of Ælfwine left no trace in the published works of *The Hobbit*, *The Lord of the Rings*, and *The Silmarillion* as edited by Christopher Tolkien, and in his later years Tolkien shifted his preference towards transmission via Númenor, Gondor, and Rivendell—though this left unexplicit the subsequent route from Middle-earth to modern times. Tolkien even toyed with the idea of explaining contradictions between his Elvish mythology and real-world cosmology on the grounds of 'Mannish' error in the course of transmission; but this would have been a strange place to end up, with a mythology presented as knowingly false.

In *The Lord of the Rings* and afterwards, Rivendell and Gondor—especially the library at Minas Tirith—also came to be specified as the repository of hobbit learning. At the end of *The Hobbit*, we see Bilbo 'sitting in his study writing his memoirs', which he thinks of calling 'There and Back Again, a Hobbit's Holiday', and the title-page inscription to early editions of *The Hobbit*, written in runes, describes the book as being 'the record of a year's journey made by Bilbo Baggins of Hobbiton, compiled from his memoirs by J. R. R. Tolkien'. From this initial idea, little more than a *jeu d'esprit* (*The Hobbit* is not, of course, a first-person narrative), came the greatly enlarged concept in *The Lord of the Rings* of 'The Red Book of Westmarch', a compendium of hobbit and Elvish lore founded on Bilbo's own collections and memoirs and augmented by Frodo's composition of 'The Downfall of the Lord of the Rings and the Return of the King'. (It seems to take Frodo somewhere between one and two years to write this: this may be a self-reflexive joke on Tolkien's part, whose own composition of *The Lord of the Rings* took well over a decade). More information about the Red Book of Westmarch was given in the preface to *The Adventures of Tom Bombadil* (1962) and the 'Note on the Shire Records' which was added to the second edition of *The Lord of the Rings* in 1966.

Editing and translating were at the heart of Tolkien's professional life as a scholar of Old and Middle English, and several of his medieval translations have been posthumously published (for example, of *Beowulf* and *Sir Gawain and the Green Knight*). So it is perhaps not surprising that, just as Tolkien became increasingly preoccupied with questions of transmission and preservation, so he also grew more and more committed to the idea that the texts he wrote (and hoped to publish) should be presented as ancient, translated texts, rather than originating with a modern, omniscient author.

In many respects, this is a brilliant conceit, superbly carried through by an author uniquely well placed to do so; it enables Tolkien, for example, to explain the variations between the first and second editions of *The Hobbit* in terms of Bilbo's own revisions to his memoirs. But there are a number of problems too, and these come to a head in the final Appendix F of *The Lord of the Rings*. The first set of problems concerns the status of *The Lord of the Rings* as a narrative, as the story is told by (seemingly) an omniscient third-person narrator; it is not told by Frodo as a first-person narrator, let alone as a first-person narrator who may not be wholly reliable. In a footnote added to the second edition of *The Lord of the Rings*, Tolkien flirts with the idea of Frodo being in some respects an unreliable narrator: in order to explain an apparent error in the first edition, the note states that '[Frodo's] limited acquaintance with Sindarin' may have 'misled' him in his representation of the language of Lothlórien. But this is a dangerous suggestion, with the potential to undermine the narrative as a whole. The inscription on the title-pages of *The Lord of the Rings*, written in runes and *tengwar*, proclaims that the work is 'translated from the Red Book of Westmarch by John Ronald Reuel Tolkien'. But is *The Lord of the Rings* literally meant to be a translation from the Red Book, or is it perhaps a modern retelling or novelization based on its contents (which is perhaps what is suggested by *The Hobbit*'s looser phrasing of 'compiled from his memoirs')? These uncertainties have been created by Tolkien's increasing conviction that his works should be construed as old books with their own history of transmission—and not as modern omniscient narratives.

The second set of problems arises at precisely the point at which Tolkien is strongest: in the representation of languages. Appendix F expounds the principles of translation in a programmatic way, explaining that 'in presenting the matter of the Red Book, as a history for people of today to read, the whole of the linguistic setting has been translated as far as possible into terms of our own times', so that while 'languages alien to the Common Speech have been left in their original form' (such as Elvish place-names), 'the Common Speech, as the language of the Hobbits and their narratives, has inevitably been turned into modern English'. Again, from many points of view, this makes good linguistic sense, and Tolkien carries through the conceit with typical philological rigour—though it is an irony that Westron or Common Speech, in which the text is supposedly written, is far from being the most well-developed language in Middle-earth in terms of linguistic invention.

But like the whole idea of the Red Book of Westmarch, this position is also an after-the-event (or during-the-event) justification or rationalization. Tolkien didn't begin writing *The Lord of the Rings* with this set of linguistic policies in place. Just as he claims that the word *hobbit* is really a translation of Westron *kuduk*, so Tolkien reports that he has 'translated all Westron names according to their senses'. He gives some examples: the place called Rivendell was really called *Karningul* in the Common Speech, he says, and Sam Gamgee was really called *Ban*, a shortening of *Banazîr*. But for a reader who has enjoyed the 1,000 pages of *The Lord of the Rings* (and perhaps *The Hobbit* before that), 'Rivendell' is likely to have become a name of enchantment and special homeliness; the revelation that it was in fact called *Karningul* is in danger of taking something away from the reader emotionally, rather than adding something. It is not a person called 'Ban' that the reader has come to care about—it's Sam.

Tolkien continued to worry away at the problems presented by this fiction of translation, and it may be that no fully consistent way through his competing priorities was possible. The fundamental idea of presenting *The Lord of the Rings* (and *The Hobbit*) as a translation from an ancient manuscript is undoubtedly powerful, and Tolkien had been committed to such frameworks from the time of his earliest mythological writings. But inevitably, as soon as the conceit becomes rigid (as it does in the appendices to *The Lord of the Rings*), difficulties start to present themselves—difficulties which are especially acute for a writer who invests so much value in the power and aesthetics of invented languages.

Chapter 6
Sources

Modern medievalism

Most works of medieval literature have not been read continuously from the time of the Middle Ages to the time of the present. Although there are some exceptions to this, such as the writings of Chaucer, most medieval works had to be 'rediscovered', as the contents of old manuscripts were printed, edited, and translated, mostly in the 19th century. *Beowulf*, for example, was first published in full in 1815, and *Sir Gawain and the Green Knight* in 1839. And what was true of medieval literature was even more true of medieval language: the secure knowledge of medieval languages was the result of 19th-century labours, as part of Tolkien's discipline of philology.

This rediscovery of medieval language and literature led to creative writers—poets, novelists, and dramatists—turning to these newly available materials to create modern works that were consciously 'medievalist', whether in terms of plot, setting, ethics, language, or style. 'New-old' was the word that Alfred Tennyson, the Poet Laureate, used to describe his own portrait of King Arthur, and Arthurian legend was undoubtedly the most favoured of source materials. But writers also made new literature out of texts from the Anglo-Saxon period and in Old Norse, as well as other medieval materials; and medievalism in literature was accompanied by similar movements in other fields, especially art and architecture. Often, such medievalism could have a political significance, in debates about democracy, or individual rights, or Christian charity, as writers and thinkers looked back to what they saw as a better time, prior to the present era of industrialism and alienation.

Tolkien is a supremely medievalist writer. As a professional scholar of medieval language and literature, he knew the sources exceptionally well, and in his own writings he sought to carry over and redeploy many elements from the literature he loved, in order to create his own 'new-old' works. This is why an awareness of Tolkien's source materials is so important: his creative processes, and his relation to his sources, were often qualitatively different from the more common case of writers who have been only moderately or unconsciously influenced by their reading. His was a deliberate act of adoption and adaptation, and the revolutionary nature of what he was doing should not be overlooked: he was not simply retelling medieval stories (as modern Arthurian writers such as Tennyson were doing), but rather he was making a new kind of literature out of medieval ingredients. Tolkien drew especially from his knowledge of Old English, Middle English, and Old Norse; but texts in other, non-Germanic languages were also important to him, including Finnish, Welsh, and medieval Latin.

A consideration of Tolkien's sources should not, however, lead to a neglect of his own creative artistry. To identify a source is not at all the same thing as to understand the literary work which that source has influenced, as Tolkien himself insisted in his essay 'On Fairy-Stories'. Nor should the piecemeal approach of source study lead to a failure to appreciate the magnitude of Tolkien's undertaking or the creative intelligence with which he carried it through. And finally, even for such a medievalist writer as Tolkien, we should not fall into the trap of thinking that there must be a source for everything: as the narrator of *The Hobbit* remarks of

Bilbo's unprophesied arrival at Lake-town, 'no songs had alluded to him even in the obscurest way'.

Tolkien was not exclusively a medievalist, either. His initial training was in Classics, and his knowledge of Latin and Greek literature was profound. He was also well read in post-medieval literature, from Shakespeare to contemporary fiction. The notion that Tolkien read little in the field of modern literature is misguided; among his unpublished papers, for example, are a set of notes on part of James Joyce's *Finnegans Wake*. But the important question here is not so much what books did Tolkien read, as rather what works had a major influence on his own creative writing?

Medieval language and literature

Old English, Middle English, and Old Norse are the three most important literatures for us to consider. One curiosity of Tolkien's engagement with these literatures, however, is that, even though he read very widely, he tended to focus on a small number of key, significant texts (often with legendary content), paying especial attention to their language. This is especially the case for Old English: as Professor of Anglo-Saxon at Oxford, it is notable—though not untypical of the scholarship of his period—how little Tolkien had to say about the religious prose that makes up a significant portion of Old English literature, and in his lectures to students he returned again and again to a small number of philologically rich poems. Tolkien valued these works not only for their antiquity, and the fascination of their language, but also for their sophistication and subtlety: he argued, for example, that it was more appropriate to refer to the fighters in *Beowulf* as 'knights' than as 'warriors', and he was adamant that Anglo-Saxon culture, pre-1066, was 'relatively advanced and artistic' compared to the 'crude and semi-barbaric Normans'. Even as an undergraduate he thought that the 'modern thirst for the 'authentically primitive'' was 'prob[ably] unwholesome'.

Middle English was the most continuous presence in his academic life and became his main professional responsibility after he switched to being Professor of English Language in 1945. Although he spent many years on a never completed edition of Chaucer, it was the anonymous poems *Pearl* and *Sir Gawain and the Green Knight* (thought to be by the same author) which most inspired him creatively, with their metrical skill, lexical density, and habitation in a world that embraced both Christian piety and the borders of Faërie. *Pearl* tells the story of a dreamer who, mourning the loss of his young daughter, is granted a vision of heaven and the new Jerusalem, and Tolkien's poem 'The Nameless Land', first written in 1924, was 'inspired by reading *Pearl* for examination purposes': it describes a beautiful, unchanging land 'where ageless afternoon goes by | O'er mead and mound and silent mere', and it was later rewritten to identify its location as the Elvish island of Tol Eressëa. *Pearl* also became an influence on the imagining of Lothlórien: like the dreamer in the poem, the Fellowship find that a stream marks the boundary into the enchanted land, and Frodo perceives that 'no blemish or sickness or deformity could be seen in anything that grew upon the earth. On the land of Lórien there was no stain.'

But it was Old English or Anglo-Saxon that especially saturated his imagination. The influence of *Beowulf* in particular was pervasive, and its impact can be seen almost everywhere in Tolkien's writings, so intimately had he absorbed the poem. The provocation of the theft of the cup from Smaug's hoard in *The Hobbit* is obviously taken straight from *Beowulf*, as is the dragon's reaction, as it sniffs out the scent of the thief, before flying out to burn the nearby settlement. Another close parallel is the process of etiquette required to gain access to Meduseld in the chapter 'The King of the Golden Hall' in *The Lord of the Rings*, modelled on Beowulf's arrival at Heorot in the poem. The melting blades at Weathertop and the Pelennor Fields trace descent from the melting sword in Grendel's mere, as do the runic inscriptions that Elrond reads on the swords taken from the trolls' hoard in

The Hobbit. In the 'Silmarillion', the companions that abandon Túrin at his climactic dragon-fight resemble the companions that abandon Beowulf at his. On a larger scale, the *Beowulf*-poet's depiction of pre-Christian characters living in a state of monotheistic natural piety may have given Tolkien an important pointer for the presentation of religion in Middle-earth. Some connections are less obvious, though. In *The Hobbit*, for example, the illustration 'The Front Gate' shows the Running River issuing from the Lonely Mountain through a stone archway. This archway is not mentioned in the accompanying text, which refers only to a 'dark cavernous opening in a great cliff-wall'. But the source here is once again *Beowulf*, where the description of the dragon's mound includes (in Tolkien's translation) 'a stone-arch [*stānboga*] standing from whence a stream came hurrying'.

The form of the monster Grendel exerted its influence on Tolkien's own bestiary. In Grendel's eyes there can be seen an ugly light, 'most like to flame', just as in *The Hobbit* Gollum's eyes 'burned with a pale flame'. The Balrogs in *The Book of Lost Tales* have 'claws of steel', just like Grendel. And the Balrog of Moria, in *The Fellowship of the Ring*, is described uncertainly as being 'a dark form, of man-shape maybe, yet greater'—an echo of the hesitancy with which Grendel and his mother are described in *Beowulf* ('of these was one, in so far as they might clear discern, a shape as of a woman; the other, miscreated thing, in man's form trod the ways of exile, albeit he was greater than any other human thing').

Already inspired by its literature as a schoolboy, Tolkien studied Old Norse as a special option as an undergraduate, and taught the subject for the first twenty-five years of his professional life. Some of the fundamentals of his Elvish mythology are evidently modelled on Norse myth, such as the pantheon of the Valar and the Ragnarok-style conclusion narrated in the *Quenta Noldorinwa*; here, Tolkien's most important source texts are the so-called *Poetic Edda* (from the Viking period) and Snorri Sturluson's later *Prose Edda* (from the 13th century). Tolkien glossed the name of his supreme deity, Ilúvatar, as 'All-Father'—a famous soubriquet for Odin in Norse mythology.

The Hobbit represents the high-point of Tolkien's creative engagement with Old Norse, and especially the *Poetic Edda*. The names of nearly all the dwarves were taken from the poem *Völuspá* or 'The Seeress' Prophecy' (one of the texts Tolkien lectured on at Oxford), as was the name of Gandalf; and *Völuspá* also supplied the association between dwarves and 'stone doors'. The heroic journeys undertaken in the legendary poems of the *Edda* often involve a passage over wet or misty mountains and/or the traversing of a forest called Mirkwood: in *The Hobbit*, Tolkien's Mirkwood is described as 'the greatest of the forests of the Northern world', and the reader is plainly meant to identify the Mirkwood of Tolkien's tale and the Mirkwood of the *Poetic Edda* as one and the same place. The skin-changer Beorn, who metamorphoses into a ferocious bear, is partly based on a character from the Old Norse *Hrólfs saga kraka*, and Tolkien's illustration of the interior of Beorn's hall is a close copy of an illustration in an Old Norse textbook written by his former Leeds colleague, E. V. Gordon. The narrator of *The Hobbit* sometimes takes on the tone and persona of an antiquarian guide to this old northern world: 'I am afraid trolls do behave like that', he informs the reader, 'even those with only one head each', and we are told that Bilbo 'knew, of course, that the riddle-game was sacred and of immense antiquity'. When they reach the Lonely Mountain, Thorin's company turn to 'discussing dragon-slayings historical, dubious, and mythical'.

The *Poetic Edda* also supplies the second great dragon of early medieval literature, to set alongside that of *Beowulf*. The poem *Fáfnismál* tells of the killing of the dragon Fáfnir by the hero Sigurd. But both the dragon and its death are very different from those of *Beowulf*. Fáfnir is not a flying dragon, and Sigurd stabs him from below as he crawls over a pit: Tolkien's story of Túrin and Glaurung derives directly from the *Fáfnismál* model of how to kill a dragon. The poem then moves on to a verbal contest between Sigurd and the dying Fáfnir, in which the former refuses to reveal his name and speaks in riddling kennings instead. This section of *Fáfnismál* is the source for Bilbo's dialogue with Smaug ('I am Ringwinner and Luckwearer; and I am Barrel-rider'); as the narrator comments, 'This of course is the way to talk to dragons [...] No dragon can resist the fascination of riddling talk.'

But Tolkien's medieval sources did not simply give him plot devices or stage properties. Bilbo's 'riddling talk' moves us on to questions of style and language as well. Medieval genres exerted a formal or structural influence on Tolkien, as in his composition of a large body of modern poetry using the alliterative verse-form of Old English. And in his philological medievalism, Tolkien's sources also gave him individual words.

There are many words that Tolkien adopted or adapted out of medieval languages (especially Old English and Old Norse) and renovated for use in modern literature. Examples include *orc* (from the unique *Beowulf*ian word *orcnēas*, meaning 'hell-corpses' or 'demon-corpses'), *mathom* (from Old English *maððum* 'treasure'), and *ent* (from Old English *ent* 'giant'). Some are eye-catching, such as *arkenstone* (an amalgam of Old English *eorclanstān* and Old Norse *jarknasteinn* 'magnificent/supernatural gem'), while others are more unobtrusive, such as *flet* (from Old English *flet* 'floor'), the word for the tree-platforms in Lothlórien. Medieval words can appear anywhere in Tolkien's writings, in the most surprising of texts: when Father Christmas, in his letter of 1932, reports his discovery of cave-paintings of 'goblin fighters [...] sitting on drasils', the word used is Old Norse *drasill*, a specifically poetic item meaning 'horse' or 'steed'. In terms of names, *Middle-earth* itself is a medieval form, taken from Middle English *middel-erde* but related also to Old English *middangeard* and Old Norse *Miðgarðr*. Like the Old Norse dwarf names in *The Hobbit*, there is a cluster of place-names derived from Old English to be found in *The Lord of the Rings*, either direct borrowings such as *Orthanc* and *Meduseld* (both Old English words which Tolkien has turned into place-names) or creative formations such as the villages and hamlets of the Shire (for example, Nobottle and Tuckborough). The names and vocabulary of Rohan, like those of the Shire, are modelled deliberately on Old English, but those of the Shire have changed over time whereas those of Rohan still retain their Old English form; this explains why Merry later 'wrote a short treatise on *Old Words and Names in the Shire*, showing special interest in discovering the kinship with the language of the Rohirrim'.

In some cases, the medieval contribution lies in the presence of an earlier word-meaning rather than the word-form itself. A Tolkienian favourite is *reek*, from Old English *rēc*, with the older meaning 'smoke' rather than the dominant modern meaning of 'smell' (for which Tolkien often prefers *stench*, from Old English *stenc*). So, for example, a character in Tolkien's pre-'Silmarillion' *Story of Kullervo* declares 'lo, an ill reek ariseth yonder'; in *The Lord of the Rings*, Frodo sees that 'Mount Doom was burning, and a great reek rising'; and the 1950s *Annals of Aman* reference 'the reeking towers of Thangorodrim'. This below-the-surface influence from medieval language also serves to explain some of Tolkien's divergences from modern English word-order, such as the post-positioned noun in the phrase 'Théoden King' (following Old English *Ælfred cyning*, rather than *King Alfred*), or the splitting of heavy groups of adjectives (in *The Hobbit* we find 'fair words and true' and 'grim men and bad', rather than 'fair and true words' and 'grim and bad men'). The syntax of Old Norse patronymics underlies 'Thorin Thrain's son Oakenshield' (as opposed to 'Thorin Oakenshield, Thrain's son'). The shaping force of medieval language and literature is systemic in Tolkien's writings.

Folklore, fairy tale, fantasy

Tolkien insisted that he was not an expert in folklore and fairy tales, but by this he may have meant that he did not belong to the anthropological school of late Victorian folklorists such as Andrew Lang and his successors. As his essay 'On Fairy-Stories' makes clear, Tolkien was well acquainted with 19th-century collections and retellings of folk material, from Lang's 'Fairy Books' (in which he first encountered the story of Sigurd) through to the six-volume *English Dialect Dictionary* of his tutor Joseph Wright (which he declared 'indispensable'). Outside of British materials, he knew the Brothers Grimm (of course) and had a special attachment to the *Kalevala*, the assemblage of old Finnish stories gathered and versified by Elias Lönnrot (1802–84): Tolkien's career as a writer of prose narrative began with his attempt to retell Lönnrot's story of Kullervo, and the *Kalevala* bequeathed a lasting influence on the 'Silmarillion'.

The Victorian period also saw the development of the literary fairy tale as a genre—that is to say, original compositions which drew on the modes and motifs of traditional folktales but were also shaped by their authors' own priorities. The figure of George MacDonald (1824–1905) is the most important here: Tolkien's goblins in *The Hobbit* owe a great deal to MacDonald's in *The Princess and the Goblin* (1872), and *Smith of Wootton Major* started life as an aborted introduction to a new edition of MacDonald's story *The Golden Key*. The border between fairy tale and fantasy is not easy to define: although 'fantasy' as a self-conscious genre postdates *The Lord of the Rings* (at least in Britain), nonetheless in the late 19th and early 20th centuries there were other writers, also proceeding under a strong medievalist impulse, who were pioneering some of the same kinds of writing as Tolkien was later to produce. Three authors will be picked out here: Lord Dunsany, E. R. Eddison, and William Morris.

The works of Lord Dunsany (1878–1957) enjoyed considerable popularity in the first two decades of the 20th century: he published a series of story-collections of mythological and heroic tales set in imaginary lands, and he was one of the first writers to

invent a whole new pantheon of fictional gods (especially in *The Gods of Pegāna* in 1905); the early iterations of Tolkien's Valar seem to owe something to Dunsany's deities, not so much in their individual characteristics as in the very fact of their existence.
E. R. Eddison (1882–1945) published *The Worm Ouroboros* (1922) and three novels set in the imaginary world of Zimiamvia, beginning with *Mistress of Mistresses* in 1935. These are written in an extraordinary archaic prose, are heavily influenced by Old Norse (as well as by Greek and Elizabethan literature), and embody Eddison's own particular philosophy. Tolkien regarded Eddison as 'the greatest and most convincing writer of 'invented worlds' that I have read', though he was not in sympathy with Eddison's beliefs and thought his name-giving poor. Tolkien seems to have first encountered Eddison's works in the early 1940s, and we can plausibly see their impact on *The Lord of the Rings* in the presence of maps and appendices, and also, perhaps, in the preoccupation with court politics, which feature prominently in the Gondorian parts of *The Lord of the Rings*, drafted subsequent to Tolkien's first reading of Eddison.

In terms of impact on Tolkien's own writings, William Morris (1834–96) is the single most important modern writer. Although Morris became a revolutionary socialist, there are close parallels between some of his political instincts and those of Tolkien, as we will see in Chapter 7. Morris's poetic story-collection *The Earthly Paradise* (1868–70) was a major influence on *The Book of Lost Tales*, not only in the nature of its frame narrative (travellers reach a distant land, where they hear a series of stories) but also in its preoccupation with questions of (im)mortality. His long poem *Sigurd the Volsung* (1876) is one of the few modern works we know Tolkien to have lectured on at Oxford. Above all, in his 'prose romances' of the late 1880s and 1890s, Morris produced a series of prototypical stories that foreshadow Tolkien in a number of important ways. These romances begin as historical fiction, with *The House of the Wolfings* (1889) telling of the struggle of a Gothic tribe, living in Mirkwood, against the encroaching Roman

Empire, but they soon break free of their historical moorings to become pseudo-medieval narratives set in invented geographies and told in archaic prose with verse embedded (*The Story of the Glittering Plain*, from 1891, is the first of these). Several of Morris's romances are structured as long journeys, there and back again, with various encounters along the way and due attention paid to matters such as water and provisions.

For the writing of his prose romances, Morris rejected the dominant styles of contemporary English fiction and instead created a new archaic medium, constructed mostly out of Old and Middle English and Old Norse. He engaged in many of the same processes of adoption and adaptation we have just observed in Tolkien's writing: *The Water of the Wondrous Isles* (1897), for example, begins: 'Whilom, as tells the tale, was a walled cheaping-town hight Utterhay.' Tolkien's prose in *The Book of Lost Tales* is largely modelled on the style of these late romances, and includes many archaic and rare words such as *astonied*, *carle*, *rede*, and *scathe*, in addition to poetic or antique variants such as *eld* and *enow*. But as he refined the nature of his more formal, elevated prose over later decades, Tolkien mostly purged his writing of this Morrisian lexical inheritance, so that the high style of the later 'Silmarillion' was achieved more by the exclusion of contemporary or low-register words than the heavy inclusion of archaic diction. But Tolkien retained, and even increased, his preference for syntactic inversion or sentence-fronting, which became one of the most prominent features of his prose when reaching for a more elevated or emphatic style: often, a single paragraph in *The Lord of the Rings* can yield several examples, as for instance when the Fellowship pass by the great statues of the Argonath and the narrator declares that 'Giants they seemed to [Frodo]', 'Upon great pedestals [...] stood two great kings of stone', and 'Great power and majesty they still wore' (as opposed to 'They seemed giants to [Frodo]', 'Two great kings of stone stood upon great pedestals', and 'They still wore great power and majesty'). Tolkien's emphatic fronting derives ultimately from his stylistic apprenticeship under Morris.

Children's literature

The 'Golden Age' of children's literature is usually held to run from the 1860s to the 1930s, though a narrower definition restricts the key period to the two decades either side of 1900. Tolkien knew this literature well—from his own childhood, his children's reading (and his reading aloud to them), and his own continued reading as an adult.

For example, the influence on *The Hobbit* of Kenneth Grahame's *The Wind in the Willows* (1908) can be readily seen in the parallels between the cosy homes of Mole and Bilbo, and their occupants' subsequent discovery of the world beyond, and also between the two forests of the Wild Wood and Mirkwood (which was in fact called 'Wild Wood' on the first map Tolkien drew for *The Hobbit*). Another writer of anthropomorphic animal stories, Beatrix Potter, received a very high valuation by Tolkien: 'On Fairy-Stories' declares that her books 'lie near the borders of Faërie', and Tolkien and C. S. Lewis dreamed of making a pilgrimage to the Lake District to pay homage to the author. E. Nesbit's Edwardian fictions, with their intrusive magic, narratorial playfulness, and child-centred perspective, influenced a whole generation of children's writers, and Tolkien was no exception. *Roverandom* is especially Nesbitian, and possible connections might also be drawn between Nesbit's Atlantis stories (in *The Story of the Amulet*, 1906, and *The Magic World*, 1912) and Tolkien's Númenor myth, as well as, perhaps, with the magic ring in *The Enchanted Castle* (1907). The dragons in Nesbit's *The Book of Dragons* (1901)—variously loquacious, comic, and anti-typical—combined with 'The Reluctant Dragon' in Grahame's *Dream Days* (1898) to generate certain aspects of Tolkien's Smaug (in *The Hobbit*) and Chrysophylax (in *Farmer Giles of Ham*).

Kipling's *Puck of Pook's Hill* (1906) has already been mentioned for its association between elves and England, and its own version of the 'departing elves' trope. Kipling, like Tolkien, rejects the Victorian and Edwardian prettification of fairies—Puck protests against 'little buzzflies with butterfly wings and gauze petticoats' as being 'made-up things' invented by humans—and Kipling's exploration of successive stages of English history, experienced through a form of haunting or time-slip, has certain parallels with Tolkien's *The Lost Road* and *The Notion Club Papers*. Puck himself is described as being 'a small, brown, broad-shouldered, pointy-eared person with a snub nose', 'no taller' than a child's shoulder and with 'bare, hairy feet': in these respects, he seems a possible contributor to the genesis of hobbits. In his Sussex rootedness, on the other hand, he forms a parallel to Tom Bombadil, especially in the early, pre-*Lord of the Rings* poems which Tolkien composed about that figure, whom he described as 'the spirit of the (vanishing) Oxford and Berkshire countryside'. And in his antiquity, as the 'oldest Old Thing in England', Puck foreshadows not only Tom Bombadil (described by Elrond as 'older than the old') but also Treebeard (described by Gandalf as 'the oldest living thing that still walks beneath the Sun upon this Middle-earth').

Connections can be observed with other works of inter-war children's literature, especially with regard to *The Hobbit*. Beorn's relations with his animals owes a good deal to Hugh Lofting's 'Doctor Dolittle' books. Tolkien himself pointed to E. A. Wyke-Smith's *The Marvellous Land of Snergs* (1927) as an 'unconscious source-book' for hobbits themselves. And in terms of book-design, *The Hobbit*'s endpaper maps are comparable to the cartographic endpapers for Arthur Ransome's 'Swallows and Amazons' series of books. Tolkien's own children were among Ransome's enthusiastic readers, and publication of *The Hobbit* led to a correspondence between the two men.

Adventure stories

The final area of modern fiction that is worth considering is the broad category of adventure stories. Tolkien enjoyed reading science fiction, and his writings indicate a familiarity with some of the earlier, pioneering works of the genre. The *palantír*s or seeing-stones in *The Lord of the Rings* seem like something out of an H. G. Wells short story ('The Crystal Egg', perhaps), as does the round, black Stone of Erech, which is described as looking 'as though it had fallen from the sky'. The supernatural thrillers of fellow-Inkling Charles Williams left their mark on Tolkien's writings, as did C. S. Lewis's interplanetary trilogy (most explicitly in *The Notion Club Papers*).

A type of fiction that Tolkien encountered at a formative age was the so-called new romance of the 1880s onwards—lost world adventures, imperial romances, and thrillers and mysteries by authors such as H. Rider Haggard, Arthur Conan Doyle, and (a little later) John Buchan. Such fictions form one of the key ingredients that went into the making of *The Lord of the Rings*, with a hinterland behind them of 19th-century historical fiction and sensation fiction: they contributed pace and mystery, startling locations, and an appropriate band of adventurers, as Tolkien worked to turn fairy tale and myth into realist fantasy.

One element taken from such stories is the foregrounding of documentary scraps and sources, often included in facsimile form: famous examples include the maps in Robert Louis Stevenson's *Treasure Island* (1883) and Haggard's *King Solomon's Mines* (1885), the elaborate 'Sherd of Amenartas' in Haggard's *She* (1887), and the various snippets of evidence that feature in several Sherlock Holmes stories (such as 'The Dancing Men' and 'The Reigate Squire'). As we saw in Chapter 5, Tolkien takes the common trope of the found manuscript to unparalleled levels of complexity, and many textual artefacts are embedded in *The Lord of the Rings*, from the inscription on Balin's tomb to that on the Ring itself. Another element taken from adventure stories is the complication of a quest or mission being jeopardized by pursuit by enemy agents: this is given a defining realization in John Buchan's *The Thirty-Nine Steps* (1915) and is energetically adopted by Tolkien in *The Fellowship of the Ring*, where Frodo's flight from the Shire—on the run, in disguise—is made perilous by the ever-nearing approach of the Black Riders.

For a sense of just how productive the influence from adventure fiction was for Tolkien's hybrid writing, we might consider some of the possible echoes of the Sherlock Holmes stories that are to be found in *The Lord of the Rings*. Do the great sections of Gandalfian exposition, in the chapters 'The Shadow of the Past' and 'The Council of Elrond', perhaps remind readers of Holmes's explanations of how he worked out a case? Has the fog on the Barrow-downs rolled in from *The Hound of the Baskervilles*, and is the plunge of Gandalf and the Balrog modelled partly on Holmes and Moriarty at the Reichenbach Falls? In the chapter 'The White Rider', Legolas and Gimli act as Watson to Aragorn's Holmes, proposing false interpretations of the evidence before the correct view is revealed ('Can you better it?' Aragorn is asked, and he replies, just like Holmes, 'Maybe, I could [...] There are some other signs near at hand that you have not considered'). Even if influence is unprovable in individual examples, it is evident that *The Lord of the Rings* overall is indebted to the kind of literature well represented by Doyle's stories.

Adventure novels are usually male-dominated, with the main cast being a band of brothers embarking together on an expedition or mystery. This may be one reason for the low salience of female characters in Tolkien's best-known fictions, a feature which has often been remarked upon. This should not be generalized across all of Tolkien's work, however: the 'Silmarillion' (written in a different genre) features many prominent female characters, such as Lúthien and Melian, while the protagonist of the late story

Aldarion and Erendis critiques the society of Númenor in which 'all things were made for [men's] service'. But the major female characters in *The Lord of the Rings*, such as Galadriel and Éowyn, are not members of the Fellowship, any more than women are usually included in the adventuring bands of Haggard and Buchan.

In this context, though, it is worth noting that Tolkien's ideas about masculinity are often very different from those of writers such as Haggard or Buchan. One of the main narrative jokes in *The Hobbit* is precisely Bilbo's improbability as a hero and his lack of the usual heroic attributes (while he was writing the book, Tolkien toyed with the idea of having Bilbo kill Smaug, but concluded in the end that the hobbit was not dragon-slayer material, as opposed to the stern and serious Bard). In *The Lord of the Rings*, Aragorn is the closest we come to a traditional male hero, but he shows an uncertainty and humility that are not often found in his Edwardian precursors. The pacifist Frodo and the gardener Sam do not fit this mould either—Frodo tells Gandalf at the start of the story that he is 'not made for perilous quests'—and it is not easy to label or parallel the extraordinary, tender relationship that develops between the two of them. So even as he drew on the devices and excitements of adventure fiction, Tolkien was reshaping the nature of its protagonists.

It is worth ending this chapter with the further reflection that among the most important of Tolkien's sources were his own earlier writings. Over several decades of unpublished practice, Tolkien had worked out the kind of writing he wanted to produce, and how to do it. And in *The Lord of the Rings* in particular, he cannily recycled motifs, characters, and even poems from his abandoned drafts and unseen back catalogue. It is clear that Tolkien thought long and hard about the craft of narrative and the art of 'Faërie'. The false impression that Tolkien only wrote two books—*The Hobbit* and *The Lord of the Rings*—can, when allied to an excessive focus on his world-building achievements, sometimes lead to a failure to appreciate what a careful and well-practised literary craftsman he was, just as an overemphasis on his medieval credentials may lead to a neglect of his affinities with more contemporary literature. Tolkien was a unique writer, but he did not exist in a literary or historical bubble.

Chapter 7
Middle-earth

Proto-Europe

Tolkien's stories are set on Earth, our planet, in an alternative or mythical past; they do not take place in another world, real or imagined. But the name 'Middle-earth', in Tolkien's works, does not itself signify Planet Earth: that is usually called Arda. Rather, 'Middle-earth' is the name of a great landmass or continent, and Tolkien's stories are mostly set in the north-west of that landmass. (We should note Tolkien's distinctive punctuation of 'Middle-earth', with a hyphen and lower case 'e': it is not called 'Middle Earth'.)

As his mythology developed, Tolkien incorporated two great cataclysms that reshaped the (originally flat) world. The first occurred at the end of the First Age—at the climax of the events of the 'Silmarillion'. Then, the Valar entered Middle-earth and defeated Morgoth in the so-called Great Battle, and 'so great was the fury of those adversaries that the northern regions of the western world were rent asunder, and the sea roared in through many chasms, and there was confusion and great noise; and rivers perished or found new paths, and the valleys were upheaved and the hills trod down'. This is why the map in the published *Silmarillion* does not agree with the map in *The Lord of the Rings*:

the western lands of Beleriand were destroyed, so that the coastline of Middle-earth shifted eastwards.

The second cataclysm and change to the world came at the end of the Second Age, in Tolkien's myth of Númenor. Across the sea, over in the west, were originally to be found the Undying Lands of Valinor or Aman: hence in the 'Silmarillion' the Elves are able to move between the two continents, in a great migration and return. The island of Númenor (in legends developed by Tolkien in the 1930s and 1940s) lay out in the ocean between Middle-earth and Aman. Its human civilization attained unparalleled heights, but it also became filled with pride, obsessed with death, and corrupted by Sauron. When the Númenóreans attempted to set foot on the Undying Lands themselves, Ilúvatar intervened to drown their island and to change the shape of the world, so that it was made round. Aman in the west was removed from the globe. No longer was Valinor (and the Lonely Isle of Tol Eressëa) able to be accessed by travellers sailing across the sea: now it could only be reached by Elvish vessels able to find the 'Straight Road' into the west. This is the journey that is being taken by the Elves in *The Lord of the Rings*.

Although the exactness of the *Lost Tales* parallels—equating Kortirion with Warwick, for example—had long been jettisoned by the time of *The Lord of the Rings*, Tolkien seems never to have abandoned the desire to make connections between his legendarium and the medieval precursor to the modern world; Middle-earth is not, to repeat, another planet. So, for instance, Tolkien's story of Númenor is obviously a version of the myth of Atlantis, a connection made explicit in the closing statement of the text *Akallabêth* that Númenor was afterwards known as 'Atalantë in the Eldarin tongue'. Similarly, a haven of the Elves on Tol Eressëa is called Avallónë—thus supplying an origin story for the medieval legend of the Isle of Avalon.

The setting of *The Lord of the Rings* is therefore some sort of antecedent to Europe, in a time that is post-'Silmarillion' and post-Númenor: the final version of Tolkien's old world, as it were, before modern geography came into being. Tolkien's own scholarship lay in the study of the languages of north-west Europe, and the conceptual geography of Middle-earth in *The Lord of the Rings* bears a certain resemblance to medieval world-maps (so-called *mappae mundi* or 'T-O' maps), in which the world was divided into three great continents: Europe in the north, Asia in the east, and Africa in the south. The map of Middle-earth in *The Lord of the Rings* is centred on proto-Europe, but there are labels in the east and the south to mark the beginnings of Rhûn (Elvish for 'east') and Harad (Elvish for 'south'). This is one reason for the representation of the inhabitants of the east and the south in that work according to medieval stereotypes, such as the bestiary-style 'oliphaunt' that Sam sees. That these compass-point associations are governed by the proto-historical mode of *The Lord of the Rings*, and are not unchanging in Tolkien's concept of Arda, is demonstrated by the contrast with the more mythical 'Silmarillion', in which the throne of Morgoth lies in the north, and Elves and Men both have their origins in the east, far beyond the lands of Beleriand. There are several hints too of the untold stories of Middle-earth outside of the north-west: so, for example, of the Istari or wizards, who included Gandalf and Saruman, it is said in the work *Of the Rings of Power and the Third Age* that some 'went into the east of Middle-earth, and do not come into these tales', and a late note by Tolkien on the Istari acknowledges that 'these legends are North-centred'. At the Council of Elrond, Aragorn relays that he has 'crossed many mountains and many rivers, and trodden many plains, even into the far countries of Rhûn and Harad where the stars are strange'.

We are told that Bilbo 'loved maps, and in his hall there hung a large one of the Country Round with all his favourite walks marked on it in red ink'. The endpaper map of Wilderland in *The Hobbit* and the map of Middle-earth in *The Lord of the Rings* (the latter drawn by Christopher Tolkien, in fact, and included in

83

early editions as a two-colour fold-out) are two of the most evocative artefacts to emerge from Tolkien's Middle-earth labours. They were not wholly unprecedented in the making of 'secondary worlds'—such maps can be found in Morris's *The Sundering Flood* (1897) and Eddison's *Mistress of Mistresses* (1935), among others—but their impact and fascination is undeniable. Tolkien himself had been producing a series of maps or charts for his mythology since the days of the early 'Silmarillion', with the cosmographical drawings of the *Ambarkanta* in the 1930s a further development (in which one can see very clearly what a small part of Middle-earth Beleriand comprises). The map of *The Lord of the Rings* is full of places not visited in the story or even mentioned in the text; it is only from the map, for example, that we learn that Bilbo's stone trolls are to be found in a wood called 'Trollshaws'. The importance of maps—not just as reference devices but as generators of mood and verisimilitude—is a significant part of Tolkien's art as a 'sub-creator'. They are yet another example of Tolkien's genre-making originality in *The Lord of the Rings*.

Landscape and environment

Working hard for his friend, C. S. Lewis wrote not one but two reviews of *The Hobbit* when it was first published. One, as we have seen, celebrated Tolkien's 'nose for an elf'; the other praised *The Hobbit* as a book which 'admits us to a world of its own—a world that seems to have been going on long before we stumbled into it'. By the time *The Lord of the Rings* was published, Tolkien had invested four decades of creative endeavour into the imagining of Middle-earth and Valinor, and his success in what is now called 'world-building' is generally acknowledged to be unsurpassed, certainly as the product of a single creative mind. But his activities as a world-builder are not evenly distributed, and inevitably they reflect his own instincts and interests. So, as we have seen, Tolkien's Middle-earth is exceptionally detailed in terms of language and nomenclature; but it is less well developed with regard to, say, economics or agriculture. Architecture and material culture perhaps fall somewhere in the middle. There are inevitable gaps in terms of depicting an entire society or even world; W. H. Auden, for example, was bothered by the lack of pets in *The Lord of the Rings*.

The clarity and specificity of Tolkien's landscape writing is remarkable. Even as it takes us through a series of landscape-types (forests, mountains, rivers, plains, and so on), *The Lord of the Rings* goes far beyond the generic or unparticularized settings of its medieval or fairy-tale antecedents: this is another aspect of Tolkien's conversion of earlier literary forms into a new kind of fiction. Thanks to Tolkien's artistry, many readers have felt as if what is being described are real, idiosyncratic locations, and neither bland stage-sets nor overly ostentatious imaginings. This sense is established early in the work, in the lengthy account of the hobbits' journey out of the Shire: the narrator tells us, for example, that 'they went down the slope, and across the stream where it dived under the road, and up the next slope, and up and down another shoulder of the hills'; or elsewhere, 'the woods on either side became denser; the trees were now younger and thicker; and as the lane went lower, running down into a fold of the hills, there were many deep brakes of hazel on the rising slopes at either hand'. *The Lord of the Rings* is full of this sort of writing, where there is no symbolic meaning to the landscape being described: as readers we are, in effect, being invited to discover the slopes, streams, and woods of Middle-earth as places to be valued and enjoyed in and of themselves. To use one of C. S. Lewis's favoured words, the landscapes of Tolkien's great work have the *anfractuosity* of real life about them—complex, sinuous, unpredictable.

One field of knowledge close to Tolkien's heart, to set alongside language, was botany. Middle-earth is distinguished by its abundant flora, from the healing *athelas* and memorial *symbelmynë* to the Elvish *elanor* and *niphredil*. The *mallorn* trees of Lothlórien are one of the great natural spectacles of the book, and Sam's *mallorn* back home in the Shire grows from being merely 'the wonder of the neighbourhood' to eventually 'one of the finest in the world'.

Trees were central to Tolkien's imagination. The Two Trees of Valinor—whose light is preserved in the Silmarils—are fundamental to his 'Silmarillion' mythology, and the White Tree of Gondor becomes an important motif in *The Return of the King*. 'Nobody cares for the woods as I care for them', laments Treebeard, and the brilliant invention of the Ents enables Tolkien to express one of his most profound loves. *The Lord of the Rings* is now recognized as a prescient environmental text, and *The Hobbit* begins 'long ago in the quiet of the world, when there was less noise and more green'. Sam is able to resist the allure of the Ring through his desire for 'the one small garden of a free gardener'. In the mythology of the 'Silmarillion', the Vala Yavanna is 'the lover of all things that grow in the earth, and all their countless forms she holds in her mind, from the trees like towers in forests long ago to the moss upon stones or the small and secret things in the mould', and in the creation of Arda 'the seeds that Yavanna had sown began swiftly to sprout and to burgeon, and there arose a multitude of growing things great and small'. This emphasis on what would now be called biodiversity, and (in Tolkien's Christian world-view) on the natural world as a good in itself, is prominent in the mythology. 'All my works are dear to me', Yavanna declares; 'All have their worth […] and each contributes to the worth of the others'.

As an environmental writer, Tolkien stands in a line from Victorian forebears such as John Ruskin and William Morris. Hobbiton possesses a water-mill, as a form of small-scale green technology, but industrialization and destruction provoke some of Tolkien's fiercest, most pain-filled writing. *The Hobbit* adopts a comic or satirical mode, writing of goblins that 'it is not unlikely that they invented some of the machines that have since troubled the world, especially the ingenious devices for killing large numbers of people at once, for wheels and engines and explosions always delighted them, and also not working with their own hands more than they could help'. *The Lord of the Rings* is more earnest and appalled. The 'sweet grass' of Rohan is 'bruised and blackened' by marching Orcs. Saruman, who 'does not care for growing things', is said to have 'a mind of metal and wheels', and he turns Isengard into a nightmare vision of industrialization, filled with 'slaves and machines': 'Iron wheels revolved there endlessly, and hammers thudded. At night plumes of vapour steamed from the vents, lit from beneath with red light, or blue, or venomous green.' But the worst shock comes at the end of the book, when Frodo and Sam return to Hobbiton, for 'this was [their] own country, and they found out now that they cared about it more than any other place in the world'. Trees have been chopped down, old houses destroyed and gardens neglected, and a 'tall chimney of brick' is now 'pouring out black smoke into the evening air'. In response to Sam's view that this is 'worse than Mordor', Frodo replies that 'Yes, this is Mordor [...] Just one of its works.' The recovery and restoration of the Shire is achieved not so much by force or politics as by the healing of the natural world, hastened by the soil which Sam has been gifted by Galadriel. 'Spring surpassed [Sam's] wildest hopes', we are told, as the new year brings 'wonderful sunshine and delicious rain' and an almost otherworldly 'air of richness and growth'.

Peoples

So ubiquitous have elves, dwarves, and orcs become in later fantasy fiction and games that it is easy to forget that this is almost single-handedly due to Tolkien's influence: such distinctive, well-developed peoples were not established as a core repertoire in pre-Tolkienian romance and fairy tale.

On the subject of 'race', Tolkien's writings show competing tendencies: on the one hand, a continuing inheritance from

19th-century anthropology and imperial romance, and on the other, a keen awareness of the perils of 20th-century ideology (though, strictly speaking, the peoples of Middle-earth, such as Elves and Dwarves, should be regarded as different species, not different races, and Tolkien sometimes used 'kindred' or 'folk' as alternative terms). His personal writings are explicit on his opposition to apartheid and anti-Semitism: confronted by ideological inquiries from a proposed German publisher of *The Hobbit* in 1938, he responded that he had no belief in 'the wholly pernicious and unscientific race-doctrine' that led to the persecution of Jews. In his 1955 lecture on 'English and Welsh', Tolkien asserted that 'language is the prime differentiator of peoples—not of 'races', whatever that much-misused word may mean in the long-blended history of western Europe'.

Nonetheless, both the 'Silmarillion' and *The Lord of the Rings* are at times structured by systems of ethnic or racial classification: the different types of Men (for example, Númenóreans, Dunlendings, Rohirrim), the three 'breeds' of Hobbits (Stoors, Harfoots, and Fallohides), and the multiple subdivisions of Elves. Moreover, to 21st-century readers, Tolkien's depictions of Orcs ('swart' and 'slant-eyed' in appearance, and armed with 'scimitars'), and also of the inhabitants of the east and south of Middle-earth ('Easterlings' and 'Swertings') may suggest some of the racial stereotypes of his own period, in addition to those of his medieval sources. There are some statements too that seem to indicate the hereditary transmission of non-physical traits: for example, the narrator states that 'even in Bilbo's time the strong Fallohidish strain [of being 'bolder and more adventurous'] could still be noted among the greater families, such as the Tooks and the Masters of Buckland', and Gandalf declares of Denethor, Steward of Gondor, that 'the blood of Westernesse [i.e. Númenor] runs nearly true in him'. In 1939, Tolkien's Oxford colleague R. G. Collingwood wrote that any 'occult entity like a racial temperament or an inheritance of acquired psychical characteristics' should not be taken seriously by historians, whereas the idea of 'folk-memory', Collingwood thought, was unexceptionable ('nothing occult; nothing inborn; simply the transmission by example and precept of certain ways of thinking and acting from generation to generation'). In 'English and Welsh', Tolkien is insistent that there is no value in the 'modern myth' of Celts and Teutons as two groups 'fixed not only in shape' but also 'endowed even in the mists of antiquity, as ever since, with [...] peculiarities of mind and temper'. But *The Lord of the Rings* does sometimes seem to suggest certain 'peculiarities of mind and temper', and it is not always clear which of Collingwood's two paradigms is at work.

The Lord of the Rings does, however, also probe repeatedly at questions of xenophobia and hostility. Early in *The Fellowship of the Ring*, the Elf Gildor warns the hobbits that 'The wide world is all about you: you can fence yourselves in, but you cannot for ever fence it out'. When the hobbits arrive at Bree, we learn that the Shire-folk call the Bree-folk 'Outsiders', and the Bree-folk call the Shire-folk the same. Beyond the Shire, it seems to be Men who are especially prone to prejudice: 'I do not feel too sure of this Elvish Lady and her purposes', says Boromir, and elsewhere he is dismissive of 'these elves and half-elves and wizards'.

Tolkien's great work is also a story of co-operation and discovery. This is most obvious in the composition of the Fellowship itself and the friendship of Gimli and Legolas, but also in Sam's encounter with the world beyond his home and his movement beyond the narrow horizons of his Shire upbringing: seeing a dead Southron, Sam 'wondered what the man's name was and where he came from; and if he was really evil of heart, or what lies or threats had led him on the long march from his home; and if he would not really rather have stayed there in peace'. When the distrustful Gimli looks into Galadriel's eyes, 'it seemed to him that he looked suddenly into the heart of an enemy and saw there love and understanding'. The book ends with two 'mixed' or intercultural marriages, as a promise for the future: Aragorn and Arwen, and Faramir and Éowyn.

Few of the peoples of Middle-earth are associated with an inalienable homeland: migration and movement are baked into their histories, from the first hobbits crossing the Baranduin to found the Shire, to the back-history of the Rohirrim moving south from an earlier habitation near Mirkwood. At Bree we learn that a number of migrants from the south are on the move, 'looking for lands where they could find some peace'. The plot of *The Hobbit* turns on Thorin Oakenshield's band of dwarves attempting to regain their old home at the Lonely Mountain. The history of Beleriand in the First Age is full of the movement of peoples. The earliest title for 'The Fall of Gondolin' was in fact 'Tuor and the Exiles of Gondolin', and one of the 'Silmarillion' works that Tolkien developed after *The Lord of the Rings* was called *The Wanderings of Húrin*. At the centre of the 'Silmarillion' lies the exile of the Noldor from Aman: the final, westward departure of the Elves from Middle-earth is thus both a return and an abandonment.

Just as it takes us through the myriad landscapes of Middle-earth, so *The Lord of the Rings* also explores a series of different cultures. *The Fellowship of the Ring* offers Moria and Lothlórien—the cultures of Dwarves and of Elves—and then we encounter Ents early in *The Two Towers*. After that, *The Two Towers* and *The Return of the King* take us deeper and deeper into the human societies of Middle-earth, especially Rohan and Gondor. The relative degrees of attention here are worth noting and seem to signal a shift in Tolkien's focus in the early 1940s, from Elves to Men. The first twenty years or so of his work as a writer (from *The Book of Lost Tales* to the 'Silmarillion' works of the mid-1930s) are centred on Elves, with little interest in Men—or at least little interest in the systems or societies of Men, as opposed to individual protagonists such as Beren and Tuor. But a major change comes over the orientation of his writing with the invention of the myth of Númenor and then the writing of *The Lord of the Rings*.

The massive development of the history of the Númenóreans in Middle-earth was mostly worked out during the writing of *The Lord of the Rings*, and this increasing 'Mannishness' also dominates its appendices. In some respects, what this amounts to is a new beginning for Tolkien as a world-builder. Just as in his earlier 'Silmarillion' writings he told the story of the Elves—their cultures, genealogies, and battles—so now he started all over again and told the story of Men. This continues into his works of the 1950s and 1960s: alongside his return to the matter of the 'Silmarillion', a significant amount of Tolkien's attention after *The Lord of the Rings* was directed towards the elaboration of Númenor and the post-Númenórean cultures of Middle-earth. Much of this material was published in the posthumous collection *Unfinished Tales*, and it represents a fascinating new genre of pseudo-history, with essays on such topics as the kings of Númenor, the early wars of the Rohirrim, and the rivers and beacon-hills of Gondor.

Government and politics

Most of the peoples of Middle-earth are ruled by monarchies. Of course, monarchy is the system of government most commonly found in Tolkien's predecessor-texts of medieval literature and fairy tales, as well as in the Old Testament, but this tendency may well express Tolkien's own instincts as well. As he wrote in a letter to his son Christopher in 1943: 'My political opinions lean more and more to Anarchy (philosophically understood, meaning abolition of control not whiskered men with bombs)—or to 'unconstitutional' Monarchy.'

This is a private letter, written partly tongue-in-cheek, and not a measured public statement; but it provides a helpful gloss to the form of rule instituted at the end of *The Return of the King*. Once Aragorn assumes the throne of Gondor (as King Elessar), what he does with his kingly power is to remove various peoples and places from his control, so that they can thereafter live free from government or somehow govern themselves. 'The King pardoned the Easterlings that had given themselves up', we are told, 'and sent them away free, and he made peace with the peoples of Harad; and the slaves of Mordor he released and gave to them all the lands about Lake Núrnen to be their own.' Similarly, 'Aragorn gave to Faramir Ithilien to be his princedom', and 'The Forest of Drúadan he [gave] to Ghân-buri-Ghân and to his folk, to be their own for ever; and hereafter let no man enter it without their leave!' Later, at Isengard, Aragorn declares that he 'will give to Ents all this valley to do with as they will, so long as they keep a watch upon Orthanc and see that none enter it without my leave', and Gandalf also promises that Aragorn will 'let Bree alone'. Finally, in an appendix to *The Lord of the Rings*, we learn that 'King Elessar issues an edict that Men are not to enter the Shire, and he makes it a Free Land under the protection of the Northern Sceptre'. As we know from his letters, Tolkien did not hold pro-imperial views—one reason, no doubt, why the Númenóreans are viewed with such ambivalence in his works—and his sympathies seem to have lain much more with the small-country patriotism of states such as Finland and Iceland. Faramir, a character with whom Tolkien identified, loves his city of Minas Tirith 'for her memory, her ancientry, her beauty, and her present wisdom', but he does not wish her to be 'feared', while *Farmer Giles of Ham* looks back to 'those days, now long ago, when this island was still happily divided into many kingdoms' and even 'villages were proud and independent still'.

There are two obvious exceptions to the monarchies of *The Lord of the Rings*: Mordor and the Shire. Sauron's land of Mordor is a totalitarian dictatorship, founded on slavery and militarism, and complete with a 'Big Brother'-style system of surveillance (Tolkien was completing *The Lord of the Rings* at the same time as Orwell was writing *Nineteen Eighty-Four*, in the immediate post-war period). As they make their way towards Mount Doom, Frodo and Sam keep hearing 'the noise of marching feet'.

As for the Shire, the Prologue to *The Lord of the Rings* tells us that it has 'hardly any 'government'', and 'families for the most part managed their own affairs', doing so in a manner that is 'generous and not greedy, but contented and moderate'. In its lack of monarchy, the Shire resembles medieval Iceland, the great political exception of medieval Europe in its republicanism and absence of a central, executive power; and the four 'farthings' of the Shire are modelled on Iceland's four 'quarters' (Old Norse *fjórðungar*), with an allusion also to the three 'ridings' or 'thirdings' of Yorkshire (Old Norse *þriðjungar*).

The Shire also bears many resemblances to the semi-medievalist utopia of William Morris's *News from Nowhere* (1891), in which England has become a garden populated by harmonious, self-regulating communities with no need for government or political parties. Tolkien had an intense dislike of centralized 'planning', as expressed in the chapter 'The Scouring of the Shire', in which the hobbits' home has been taken over by Men with a system of 'gatherers' and 'sharers', dominated by those who 'like minding other folk's business and talking big'. The chapter contains some of Tolkien's most satirical writing, as the returning travellers find the Shire governed by a written 'list of Rules' rather than the customary 'laws of free will […] ancient and just' lauded in the Prologue ('If I hear *not allowed* much oftener', Sam declares, 'I'm going to get angry'). Brian Rosebury has aptly characterized Tolkien as 'a type of Christian quasi-anarchist who rejects the claims of secular politics […] because he believes that political institutions are intrinsically coercive'. As Tolkien wrote in his 1943 letter to his son, he believed strongly that 'the most improper job of any man […] is bossing other men', and that 'not one in a million is fit for it, and least of all those who seek the opportunity'.

Chapter 8
Elegy

War

Tolkien was insistent that the Old English poem *Beowulf* is not an epic. No, he said, *Beowulf* is not an epic, but rather a 'heroic-elegiac' poem. And this compound adjective—heroic-elegiac—supplies a fine gloss to many of Tolkien's own writings. A sense of loss and mourning runs through many of his works—a sense of sorrow variously attributable to war and mortality, time and exile, and the human experience of being weak and fallen.

Tolkien's creative energies were first fully unlocked in a time of conflict, through bereavement. The devastating loss of his parents was followed by the death in battle of many of his school and college friends. As he later wrote, during his war service his 'Silmarillion' mythology came into existence through 'the desire to express [his] *feeling* about good, evil, fair, foul in some way: to rationalize it, and prevent it just festering'. Tolkien was profoundly affected by his experiences in the First World War—physically, emotionally, and psychologically—and then *The Lord of the Rings* was mostly written during the Second World War. It is not a surprise that war and battles assume such a prominent position in his stories. The first great tale that Tolkien wrote was a war story, 'The Fall of Gondolin', in which heroic last stands, straight out of early medieval poetry, are coupled with the mechanized destruction wrought by tank-like metal dragons spouting flame. Like other war writers, Tolkien had to find his own language, and 'The Fall of Gondolin' attests to a curious hybridity in style as well as content: medieval (or medievalist) words such as *byrnie*, *hauberk*, and *house-carle* sit alongside contemporary military terms such as *battalion*, *troop*, and *debouch*. The same hybridity extends to *The Lord of the Rings*, where medieval military terms include *shield-wall*, *shieldmaiden*, and *vambrace*, and coexist with modern ones such as *sortie*, *assault*, and *bivouac*.

In his modern medievalism, then, Tolkien's war-writing faces two ways, in both style and sensibility: this is the distinctive mixture that he offers his readers. Some of his works tell archaic stories of heroism, in thrilling and unironic fashion, but at other times they are also informed by a contemporary awareness that old-style heroics will not suffice or will bring insuperable problems in one way or another. The Battle of Five Armies in *The Hobbit* includes Beorn's late onslaught: 'he seemed to have grown almost to giant-size in his wrath [...] and he tossed wolves and goblins from his path like straws and feathers [...] nothing could withstand him, and no weapon seemed to bite upon him'. This is the excitement of heroic narrative. But Bilbo's reaction to the battle is the modern perspective: "Victory after all, I suppose!' he said, feeling his aching head. 'Well, it seems a very gloomy business". The verse drama *The Homecoming of Beorhtnoth Beorhthelm's Son* gives us Tolkien's reflections on the Old English poem *The Battle of Maldon*, and on what he saw as the misplaced heroics evidenced there: the character Tídwald, old and undeceived, judges Beorhtnoth's disastrous actions, which led to the defeat of the English, as being 'needlessly noble', motivated by a misguided desire 'to give minstrels matter for mighty songs'.

While 'The Fall of Gondolin' was written white-hot after Tolkien survived the Battle of the Somme, *The Hobbit*—largely composed *c.*1929–32, in the era of the war memoir—seems to present some of Tolkien's experiences in more refracted form. 'Going on from there was the bravest thing he ever did', the narrator says in a trench-like scene, as Bilbo forces himself towards his first encounter with Smaug. 'The tremendous things that happened afterwards were as nothing compared to it. He fought the real battle in the tunnel alone, before he ever saw the vast danger that lay in wait.' On 'Thror's Map', the shattered trees at the Desolation of Smaug look very like the broken stumps familiar to us from photographs and paintings of the Western Front. In *The Lord of the Rings*, Tolkien's undergraduate service in a volunteer cavalry unit, King Edward's Horse, may lie behind his interest in the horses and manoeuvres of the Rohirrim ('they checked their steeds, wheeled, and came charging round'); later in the book, Frodo and Sam creep across the no man's land of Mordor, and shelter in what are effectively shell-holes (the land is 'pocked with great holes, as if [...] it had been smitten with a shower of bolts and huge slingstones').

The Lord of the Rings was begun in 1937 and completed in draft in 1948; as the writing went on, the book became more and more dominated by the Middle-earth equivalent of a world war—the War of the Ring. In the early sections there is the foreboding sense of a gathering storm, often articulated by Gandalf in Churchillian mode: Frodo wishes 'it need not have happened in my time', to which Gandalf responds that 'so do all who live to see such times. But that is not for them to decide', and later the wizard promises that 'the great storm is coming, but the tide has turned'. The notion of a whole world erupting into war reaches its climax at the end of *The Fellowship of the Ring*, in Frodo's vision from the summit of Amon Hen, where 'everywhere he looked he saw the signs of war'. Even those who survive combat in *The Lord of the Rings* do not escape unscathed. Like other fighters in the Battle of the Pelennor Fields, Merry afterwards suffers from the 'Black Shadow' or 'Black Breath', a sort of Middle-earth shell-shock ('Help me, Pippin! It's all going dark again, and my arm is so cold'). There is a resemblance here also to Frodo's sorrow and alienation at the end of the book, as he suffers from 'wounds that cannot be wholly cured': he confesses to Gandalf that 'the wound aches, and the memory of darkness is heavy on me', so that, for him, there can be 'no real going back' to his pre-war life in the Shire.

In the Second World War, Tolkien was not a combatant but a civilian (with sons in the forces), and while the book draws on his own war service for the experience of combat, it also gives attention to the civilian perspective. Alongside the human stories of evacuations and refugees, there are more trivial details such as rationing ('Pippin looked ruefully at the [...] inadequate pat of butter which was set out for him'), and Gandalf even becomes a kind of air-raid warden (as Tolkien himself did during the war), telling the people of Rohan to 'kindle no more lights or fires than barest need asked' because of the flying Nazgûl. This focus on civilian experiences, and on ordinary communities caught up in war, continues in some of his later 'Silmarillion' writings, especially the extensive collection of texts associated with Húrin and his children.

Time and loss

Tolkien wrote in a letter that he was deeply moved by 'the heart-racking sense of the vanished past'. A philologist to his core, he viewed human culture in terms of change over time. His system-making instincts often expressed themselves in chronological schemes: not only Elvish sound-changes but also multiple forms of annals and timelines. But simple chronology is not in itself 'heart-racking'. Rather, as Tolkien wrote in another letter, it is the sense of 'glimpses of a large history in the background', and of 'unattainable vistas', that provokes the emotion.

Tolkien's first major work was called *The Book of Lost Tales*, and his first version of the Númenor story was *The Lost Road*. The longest of the *Lost Tales* is 'The Fall of Gondolin', and later works include *The Fall of Arthur* and *The Fall of Númenor* (subsequently retitled *The Downfall of Númenor* or *Akallabêth*). The very names of these works—'lost', 'fall'—not only denote, factually, a 'vanished past' but also come freighted with poignancy and regret. In the poem *Beowulf*, Tolkien felt that he encountered 'a dark antiquity of sorrow'; and he was attracted instinctively to time-travel narratives, as seen in his own *Notion Club Papers*.

This sense of history and loss is one of the pre-eminent qualities that readers experience in *The Lord of the Rings* and one of the most important ways in which Tolkien's achievement as a world-builder or sub-creator is hard to parallel. The chapter 'The Council of Elrond', the longest in the book, is audacious in the sheer quantity of history which it presents, not least because it has already been preceded by a good deal of information in 'The Shadow of the Past'. Moreover, these chapters in no way exhaust the provision of prior history within the work; if they did, there would be no need for the appendices. Above all, the whole history of the Second Age, from the founding of Númenor to the Last Alliance, was elaborated during (and for) the writing of *The Lord of the Rings*, and it is never related at length as a narrative in its own right (unlike the stories of the First Age, which pre-existed *The Lord of the Rings* in the form of many 'Silmarillion' writings).

As the members of the Fellowship travel through Middle-earth, they stumble upon the physical remains of previous cultures, often presented with a Gothic frisson (another of Tolkien's debts to the 'lost world' stories of Haggard, Doyle, and others). On the way to Rivendell, for example, the hobbits encounter standing stones and old burial chambers on the Barrow-downs. Mount Weathertop is a ruined watch-tower, surrounded by half-hidden earthworks and the like. Approaching Moria, they come upon choked water-channels and 'the ruined walls and paving-stones of an ancient highroad', and 'A Journey in the Dark' offers a chapter-length exploration of the abandoned dwarf-halls within. At Amon Hen, Frodo follows 'the dwindling ruins of a road of long ago'. Later in the quest, as they make their way through Ithilien, Frodo and Sam follow a road 'made in a long lost time', until at last 'all signs of stonework faded, save for a broken pillar here and there, peering out of bushes at the side, or old paving-stones still lurking amid weeds and moss'. As these few examples (among many) indicate, Middle-earth is filled with broken and crumbling remains, half-hidden glimpses of a 'vanished past'.

On a number of occasions, Tolkien said that one of the main themes of his writing was death. The ache of mortality runs through many of his works and reaches its sharpest focus in Tolkien's examination of the contrastive experiences of Elves and Men. In Tolkien's mythology, as in real life, the burden of Men is that they are mortal; and the burden of Elves is that they are immortal. Tolkien's writings express the inevitably conflicted emotions that a mortal author—and a Christian—might feel towards these two conditions. When Elves, the Firstborn of the 'Children of Ilúvatar', encounter the first Men in Middle-earth, they wonder and grieve at 'the coming of death without wound' and 'the short span that was allotted to them'. The subject is explored most directly in the 1950s dialogue text *Athrabeth Finrod ah Andreth*, in which the Elf Finrod and the wise woman Andreth debate questions of mortality. As Andreth states: 'No heart of Man is content. All passing and dying is a grief to it [...] Death is an uttermost end, a loss irremediable.' Within his (pre-Christian) mythology, Tolkien developed an account of what happens to Elves who are killed—they go to the halls of the Vala Mandos—but the fate of Men remains undisclosed, as yet. Tolkien proposed the mythological idea that death is in fact a 'gift' which Ilúvatar has granted to Men, as a concomitant of their free will, and not to Elves. As he wrote in one version of *Ainulindalë*, his creation story:

> It is one with this gift of freedom that the children of Men dwell only a short space in the world alive, and are not bound to it, and depart soon whither we know not. Whereas the Eldar remain until

the end of days, and their love of the Earth and all the world is more single and poignant, therefore, and as the years lengthen ever more sorrowful.

Thus the very nature of their existence, and their contrastive dooms, brings inevitable sorrow to both Elves and Men.

The same version of *Ainulindalë* states that Ilúvatar 'willed that the hearts of Men should seek beyond the world and should find no rest therein'. This is Tolkien's transposition into Middle-earth of the Christian notion that humans are exiles on earth, with a longing for our true home in heaven. Many of the Elves of Middle-earth are in a state of exile too: they are exiles from the Undying Lands of Valinor. This is why, in Tolkien's work, the separating sea is often an emblem of sorrow, marking as it does the Elves' sojourn in 'these lands of exile' and the bittersweet nature of their final journey west-over-sea. In the original, excluded epilogue to *The Lord of the Rings*, we end in melancholic fashion with Sam hearing 'the sigh and murmur of the sea on the shores of Middle-earth'.

Fallenness, failure, pity

As a Christian, Tolkien believed intensely in the 'fallen' nature of humanity and the world—that is to say, their corruption through disobedience and sin, and their consequent instability and tendency towards evil as well as good. His letters contain repeated references to 'fallen man' and 'this fallen world'. In Tolkien's mythology, unlike in the Christian story of Genesis, the world—Arda—is compromised from the very beginning, on account of the discordant contributions of Melkor/Morgoth to the 'Music of the Ainur' which brought it into existence, so that from the start Ilúvatar's creation is 'blended with an immeasurable sorrow', and 'all things, save in Aman alone, had an inclination to evil and to perversion from their right forms and courses'. In his later 'Silmarillion' writings, Tolkien used the phrase 'Arda Marred' to characterize the nature of the fallen world, with a contrast to the longed-for state of 'Arda Unmarred' or 'Arda Healed'.

Men and Elves are fallen too, though in different ways. The fall of Man—Tolkien's equivalent of the Christian story of Adam and Eve's disobedience and their expulsion from Eden—happens offstage in his mythology, and when Men first appear in Middle-earth they tell the Elves that 'a darkness lies behind us'. The nature of the fall of the Elves is a subject which Tolkien greatly pondered on—since he had more latitude as a sub-creator—and he reached a number of possible conclusions. In his 'Silmarillion' texts, it is Melkor/Morgoth who finds the newly awakened Elves ahead of the other Valar; in the *Annals of Aman*, for example, when the Vala Oromë subsequently encounters the Elves, 'some of [them] hid themselves', just like Adam and Eve. According to Tolkien, this fundamental state of 'fallenness' might then be recapitulated in countless individual lives, actions, and histories: the *Quenta Silmarillion*, he told one correspondent, is about 'the fall of the most gifted kindred of the Elves'—that is, the Noldor—and their 'exile from Valinor'.

If we move from the 'Silmarillion' to *The Lord of the Rings*, we can see that this intense consciousness of the state of being fallen, allied with an equally keen sense of the value of pity or mercy, goes a long way towards explaining the book's compassionate, but not indulgent, morality. *The Lord of the Rings* is full of characters facing temptation, and often failing. Especially humans: it is the nine human ring-bearers who long ago succumbed to Sauron and became ring-wraiths; and of the members of the Fellowship, it is Boromir who most wishes to use the Ring for aggressive purposes. As he lies dying, Boromir's last words are, 'I have failed', to which Aragorn responds that, on the contrary, 'It is I that have failed'.

Weakness and failure run throughout *The Lord of the Rings*, and Frodo especially becomes a figure through whom Tolkien expresses some of his deepest feelings about frailty and mercy. 'Where shall I find courage?' Frodo asks early in the story, but what follows is not a clichéd transformation of Frodo into a figure of heroic stature. While an apocryphal version of Frodo's quest later springs up in the city of Minas Tirith ('Why, cousin, one of them went with only his esquire into the Black Country and fought with the Dark Lord all by himself, and set fire to his Tower, if you can believe it'), *The Lord of the Rings* itself does not purvey such glib tropes or easy fantasies. Rather, we follow a protagonist who, notwithstanding his spiritual growth, remains weak and fearful to the end. 'I am afraid,' Frodo tells Boromir at Amon Hen, 'simply afraid', and Sam confirms that 'now it's come to the point, he's just plain terrified'. To Faramir later, Frodo similarly confesses that 'I am weary, and full of grief, and afraid', and to Sam, on finally reaching Mordor, he admits, 'I am tired, weary, I haven't a hope left'.

And yet he continues, with Sam beside him. One of the virtues or qualities that Tolkien most admired was endurance, not least when grounds for hope seem to be lost. In his scholarly work, he found this in Old English and Old Norse poetry, in the figure of Beowulf or the Norse gods at Ragnarok. In his 'Silmarillion' writings, Tolkien implicitly Christianizes the idea and expresses it through the Elvish word *estel*, meaning 'hope' or (more fully) trust in the ultimate efficacy of divine providence: the Elf Finrod tells Andreth that 'the last foundation of *Estel*' is that Ilúvatar 'will not suffer Himself to be deprived of His own, not by any Enemy, not even by ourselves', but the human Andreth responds that it is 'part of our wound that *Estel* should falter and its foundations be shaken'. In *The Lord of the Rings*, though, Tolkien mostly made this courage hobbit-sized, and not legendary or theological. As Frodo and Sam labour on into Mordor, 'small but indomitable', we are told that 'their wills did not yield, and they struggled on', and that Sam 'knew all the arguments of despair and would not listen to them'.

At the climax, though, Frodo fails. He does not after all surrender the Ring at Mount Doom, and announces: 'I do not choose now to do what I came to do. I will not do this deed. The Ring is mine!' The words 'choose' and 'will' carry meaning here, signalling Frodo's moral agency. Tolkien was adamant about Frodo's failure, writing to one correspondent in 1956 that 'if you re-read all the passages dealing with Frodo and the Ring, I think you will see that not only was it *quite impossible* for him to surrender the Ring, in act or will, especially at its point of maximum power, but that this failure was adumbrated from far back'.

This brings us, then, to Gollum, the unwitting third party through whom the Ring is destroyed, and one of Tolkien's most extraordinary and profound creations—in his history, his psychology, and his unforgettable style of speech. He is a thief and a murderer whose long life has been shaped and corrupted by the influence of the Ring; but he is also an extreme case of a wicked figure who is still deemed worthy of pity and is not beyond the reach of grace. Gollum's is 'a sad story', Gandalf explains to Frodo at the start of the book: even though, as a hobbit, he was not 'wholly ruined' by possession of the Ring, nonetheless he 'hated it and loved it, as he hated and loved himself'. In response to Frodo's initial opinion that it was a 'pity' that Bilbo did not kill Gollum when he had the chance to do so (in *The Hobbit*), Gandalf is insistent that, on the contrary, 'it was Pity that stayed his hand', and that although he has 'not much hope that Gollum can be cured before he dies', still 'there is a chance of it'. Later, Frodo perceives the truth of this: 'For now that I see him, I do pity him.'

Tolkien's introductory synopsis to *The Return of the King* summarizes how, in the course of Book IV in *The Two Towers*, 'Frodo tamed Gollum and almost overcame his malice', but in the end 'Gollum fell back into evil'. The heartbreaking moment, where Gollum's fate hangs in the balance, comes as the travellers rest on their ascent of Cirith Ungol:

Slowly putting out a trembling hand, very cautiously [Gollum] touched Frodo's knee—but almost the touch was a caress. For a fleeting moment, could one of the sleepers have seen him, they would have thought that they beheld an old weary hobbit, shrunken by the years that had carried him far beyond his time, beyond friends and kin, and the fields and streams of youth, an old starved pitiable thing.

But the moment is only 'fleeting'. Sam awakes and, misconstruing Gollum's gesture, disastrously accuses him of being a 'sneak'. The possibility of change or repentance for Gollum vanishes and never arises again. Yet even on the very slopes of Mount Doom, Sam cannot bring himself to 'strike this thing lying in the dust, forlorn, ruinous, utterly wretched'. Gollum is one of the absolutely central characters of the book, not just for the plot but also as a figure of intense emotion and suffering, and as a focus for Tolkien's preoccupation with fallenness, pity, and agency.

Frodo's experience as ring-bearer changes him deeply. On the journey to Mount Doom he forswears weapons, and after the Battle of Bywater, in 'The Scouring of the Shire', we are told that 'his chief part had been to prevent the hobbits [...] from slaying those of their enemies who threw down their weapons'. In the same chapter, Frodo wants to 'save' the collaborator Lotho, not punish him (an attitude incomprehensible to his companions), and he wishes also to spare Saruman: 'He is fallen, and his cure is beyond us; but I would still spare him, in the hope that he may find it.' Frodo is too much changed, in fact, to find rest back home in the Shire.

Eucatastrophe

But we should not end with sorrow and weakness. As a Christian, Tolkien believed not only in the fallenness of humanity (and, by extension, of other created beings) but also in the possibility—or, indeed, the reality—of divine intervention and salvation. As we have seen, he even implanted the idea of the 'Old Hope' or 'Great Hope' of Christ's incarnation into his late 'Silmarillion' writings, and he believed that fairy tales possessed value precisely because they foreshadowed or echoed this ultimate 'good news'.

'Eucatastrophe' is the word that Tolkien coined for this, and which he advocated in his essay 'On Fairy-Stories':

> The consolation of fairy-stories, the joy of the happy ending: or more correctly of the good catastrophe, the sudden joyous 'turn' (for there is no true end to any fairy-tale): this joy, which is one of the things which fairy-stories can produce supremely well, is not essentially 'escapist', nor 'fugitive'. In its fairy-tale—or otherworld—setting, it is a sudden and miraculous grace: never to be counted on to recur. It does not deny the existence of *dyscatastrophe*, of sorrow and failure: the possibility of these is necessary to the joy of deliverance; it denies (in the face of much evidence, if you will) universal final defeat and in so far is *evangelium*, giving a fleeting glimpse of Joy, Joy beyond the walls of the world, poignant as grief.

Tolkien then proceeds to make a grander claim for the idea of eucatastrophe: the supreme sudden reversal and happy ending, he argues, comes in the story of Jesus, when the seeming defeat of the Crucifixion is triumphantly undone by his Resurrection three days later. This is 'the greatest and most complete conceivable eucatastrophe'. So for Tolkien, as a Catholic, eucatastrophic narratives have a distinctively Christian shape.

This helps us to understand the echoes and overtones that cluster around the climax of *The Lord of the Rings*. The rescue of Sam and Frodo by the eagles is a moment of pure eucatastrophic joy—'a happiness that brings tears, like the thrill of the sudden turn for good in a dangerous tale', as a character in *The Notion Club Papers* puts it. But Tolkien is also encouraging us to see some sort of Christian message in play as well. It cannot be a coincidence that, as an appendix tells us, the Ring was destroyed on 25 March—that is, in the Christian calendar, the date of the Annunciation, when the angel Gabriel appeared to Mary to announce the good news of the Incarnation. Tolkien is setting up some sort of parallel between the destruction of the Ring and the Annunciation—the latter being, for a Christian such as Tolkien, the crucial turning point in human affairs, when God intervened to bring about a change. An eagle brings an extraordinarily Psalm-like song to Minas Tirith ('Sing and rejoice, ye people of the Tower of Guard'). And when Sam meets Gandalf again at the Field of Cormallen, he asks simply and powerfully: 'Is everything sad going to come untrue?'

This promise of sad things coming untrue—of a joy that is 'poignant as grief'—is the hope that Tolkien holds forth, and holds onto, in the midst of his stories of failure and loss. Such a hope does not turn *The Lord of the Rings*, or the writings of the 'Silmarillion', into Christian allegory: they remain a new, special form of fairy tale or mythology. But one can see why Tolkien was adamant that his work was fundamentally Christian, in spite of the paucity of explicit references to his faith.

A fitting work to end with, therefore, is the short story *Leaf by Niggle*, probably written in 1942 and first published in 1945. A Christian fairy tale, showing the influence of George MacDonald and of Tolkien's own essay 'On Fairy-Stories', it is both the most allegorical and the most autobiographical of all of Tolkien's stories. The painter Niggle, working on a grand picture of a tree, is a procrastinator and perfectionist, whose social and neighbourly duties compromise his artistic dedication, and whose artistic dedication compromises his attention to his duties; meanwhile, unsympathetic onlookers either are oblivious of his creative endeavours or dismiss them as 'private day-dreaming'. It is not hard to see this as a self-portrait of Tolkien as artist, academic, and family man; and *Leaf by Niggle* was written when he had no certainty at all that he would ever be able to complete *The Lord of the Rings*, let alone find an audience for it or the rest of his writings. Would *The Lord of the Rings* and the 'Silmarillion' be left to languish unfinished and neglected, like Niggle's tree picture?

But there is a sudden, eucatastrophic turn in *Leaf by Niggle*. After his death, and having passed through a kind of purgatory, Niggle finds that his great canvas of a tree has somehow been completed and brought to life, and it is now a part of the landscape:

> He gazed at the Tree, and slowly he lifted his arms and opened them wide.
>
> 'It's a gift!' he said. He was referring to his art, and also to the result; but he was using the word quite literally.

Not only that, but other travellers in the same landscape come to value Niggle's tree, so that it proves to be 'very useful indeed [...] as a holiday, and a refreshment', and for some people even 'it works wonders'.

We can interpret the tree as either *The Lord of the Rings*, or now—in the light of posthumous publications—as Tolkien's whole body of writings. And the astounding reach and success of Tolkien's work, led by *The Lord of the Rings*, can itself now be seen as a eucatastrophic story, in terms of both literary and cultural history and also Tolkien's own life. 'Nothing has astonished me more', he said, 'than the welcome given to *The Lord of the Rings*', and he wrote to one correspondent that 'it remains an unfailing delight to me to find my own belief justified: that the 'fairy-story' is really an adult genre, and one for which a starving audience exists'. This is the unexpected turn in modern culture which Tolkien achieved, bringing to millions of readers Fantasy, Recovery, Escape, and Consolation.

References

Chapter 1: Reading Tolkien

'this is not a work […]': quoted in Tom Shippey, *The Road to Middle-earth*, rev. ed. (London: HarperCollins, 2005), p. 1.

'liked to have books filled […]': J. R. R. Tolkien, *The Lord of the Rings*, rev. ed. (London: HarperCollins, 2004), p. 7.

Chapter 2: Life and work

'stood [him] in good stead […]': J. R. R. Tolkien, *Letters*, ed. Humphrey Carpenter with Christopher Tolkien (London: George Allen and Unwin, 1981), p. 85 (no. 73).

'written in [his] life-blood': Tolkien, *Letters*, p. 122 (no. 109).

'exposed [his] heart to be shot at': Tolkien, *Letters*, p. 172 (no. 142).

'expos[ing] my world of imagination […]': Tolkien, *Letters*, p. 366 (no. 282).

'necessary to salvation': J. R. R. Tolkien, *The Monsters and the Critics and Other Essays*, ed. Christopher Tolkien (London: George Allen and Unwin, 1983), p. 225.

'would always rather try […]': Tolkien, *The Monsters and the Critics*, p. 224.

'unforgettable experience' and 'the voice was the voice of Gandalf': quoted in Humphrey Carpenter, *J. R. R. Tolkien, A Biography* (London: George Allen and Unwin, 1977), p. 138.

'incoherent and often inaudible': Kingsley Amis, *Memoirs* (London: Hutchinson, 1991), p. 53.

'puckish fisherman [...]': Robert Burchfield, 'My Hero: Robert Burchfield on J. R. R. Tolkien', *Independent Magazine* 4 March 1989, p. 50.

'crimes of omission': Tolkien, *Letters*, p. 301 (no. 223).

'creation from philology': T. A. Shippey, 'Creation from Philology in *The Lord of the Rings*', in Mary Salu and Robert T. Farrell (eds), *J. R. R. Tolkien: Scholar and Storyteller* (Ithaca: Cornell University Press, 1979), pp. 286–316.

'the chief biographical fact' and 'astonishe[d]': Tolkien, *Letters*, p. 257 (no. 199).

'author of the century': Tom Shippey, *J. R. R. Tolkien: Author of the Century* (London: HarperCollins, 2000).

Chapter 3: Stories

'I don't know [...]': Carpenter, *J. R. R. Tolkien*, p. 83.

'In a hole in the ground [...]': J. R. R. Tolkien, *The Hobbit, or There and Back Again*, anniversary ed. (London: Unwin Hyman, 1987), p. 11; Tolkien, *Letters*, p. 215 (no. 163).

Etymology of *hobbit*: Tolkien, *The Lord of the Rings*, pp. 1137–8.

'I cordially dislike allegory [...]': Tolkien, *The Lord of the Rings*, p. xxiv.

Quenta Eldalien: J. R. R. Tolkien, *Sauron Defeated: The End of the Third Age. The History of the Lord of the Rings, Part Four*, ed. Christopher Tolkien, The History of Middle-earth 9 (London: HarperCollins, 1992), p. 303.

'Then Daddy began a story [...]': J. R. R. Tolkien, *Farmer Giles of Ham*, ed. Christina Scull and Wayne G. Hammond, 50th anniversary edition (London: HarperCollins, 1999), p. 81.

'took to writing poetry [...]': Tolkien, *The Hobbit*, p. 254.

'the High Elves of the West': Tolkien, *The Hobbit*, p. 51.

'the Northern world': Tolkien, *The Hobbit*, pp. 119, 246.

'the North': Tolkien, *The Hobbit*, pp. 51, 241.

'Now you know enough [...]': Tolkien, *The Hobbit*, p. 12.

'long ago one of [Bilbo's] Took ancestors [...]': Tolkien, *The Hobbit*, p. 12.

'the fellow who used to tell [...]': Tolkien, *The Hobbit*, p. 14.

'carry away people [...]': Tolkien, *The Hobbit*, p. 29.

'old castles with an evil look [...]': Tolkien, *The Hobbit*, p. 34.

'long ago': Tolkien, *The Hobbit*, p. 13.

'as one long Saga [...]': Tolkien, *Letters*, p. 139 (no. 126).

'the Old Hope' and 'the One will himself enter [...]': J. R. R. Tolkien, *Morgoth's Ring. The Later Silmarillion, Part One: The Legends of Aman*, ed. Christopher Tolkien, The History of Middle-earth 10 (London: HarperCollins, 1993), p. 321.

'the Great Hope': Tolkien, *Morgoth's Ring*, p. 351.

Chapter 4: Faërie

'It smells like elves!': Tolkien, *The Hobbit*, p. 48.

'it may be many years [...]': C. S. Lewis, *Image and Imagination: Essays and Reviews*, ed. Walter Hooper (Cambridge: Cambridge University Press, 2013), p. 98.

'Faërie cannot be caught [...]': Tolkien, *The Monsters and the Critics*, p. 114.

'Fantasy, Recovery, Escape, Consolation [...]': Tolkien, *The Monsters and the Critics*, p. 138.

'quality of strangeness and wonder': Tolkien, *The Monsters and the Critics*, p. 139.

'the desire to converse with other living things': Tolkien, *The Monsters and the Critics*, p. 152.

'the love of Faery is the love of love [...]': J. R. R. Tolkien, *Smith of Wootton Major*, extended ed., ed. Verlyn Flieger (London: HarperCollins, 2005), p. 131.

'"Faery" is as necessary for the health [...]': Tolkien, *Smith of Wootton Major*, pp. 144–5.

'stories that are actually concerned [...]': Tolkien, *The Monsters and the Critics*, p. 113.

'Goblin Feet': J. R. R. Tolkien, 'Goblin Feet', in *Fifty New Poems for Children: An Anthology Selected from Books Recently Published by Basil Blackwell*, 3rd ed. (Oxford: Basil Blackwell, 1929), pp. 26–7.

'Men called King Felagund [...]': J. R. R. Tolkien, *The Silmarillion*, ed. Christopher Tolkien (London: George Allen and Unwin, 1977), p. 141.

'perilous land' and 'fair and perilous': Tolkien, *The Lord of the Rings*, p. 338.

'a vanished world', 'a light was upon it [...]', and 'he saw no colour [...]': Tolkien, *The Lord of the Rings*, p. 350.

'never before had he been [...]', 'this is more Elvish [...]', and '*inside* a song': Tolkien, *The Lord of the Rings*, p. 351.

'Here is the heart of Elvendom on earth': Tolkien, *The Lord of the Rings*, p. 352.

'in a timeless land [...]': Tolkien, *The Lord of the Rings*, p. 351.

'they could not count the days [...]': Tolkien, *The Lord of the Rings*, p. 370.

'If there's any magic about [...]': Tolkien, *The Lord of the Rings*, p. 361.

'did not (and do not) [...]' and 'they move and think swifter [...]': J. R. R. Tolkien, *The Nature of Middle-earth: Late Writings on the Lands, Inhabitants, and Metaphysics of Middle-earth*, ed. Carl F. Hostetter (London: HarperCollins, 2021), p. 90.

'great ages elapse [...]': J. R. R. Tolkien, *The Book of Lost Tales: Part II*, ed. Christopher Tolkien, The History of Middle-earth 2 (London: George Allen and Unwin, 1984), p. 281.

'as Men wax more powerful [...]': Tolkien, *The Book of Lost Tales: Part II*, p. 283.

'some of these things are sung [...]': J. R. R. Tolkien, *The Shaping of Middle-earth: The Quenta, the Ambarkanta, and the Annals, together with the earliest 'Silmarillion' and the first Map*, ed. Christopher Tolkien, The History of Middle-earth 4 (London: George Allen and Unwin, 1986), p. 165.

'If you succeed [...]': Tolkien, *The Lord of the Rings*, p. 365.

'But the Elves are sailing away still [...]' and 'Elves are sad [...]': Tolkien, *Sauron Defeated*, p. 115.

'all the Eldalië on earth [...]': Tolkien, *Morgoth's Ring*, p. 212.

'[they] find their supersession [...]': Tolkien, *Morgoth's Ring*, p. 342.

'Once upon a time [...]': Tolkien, *Letters*, p. 144 (no. 131).

'mythology for England': Carpenter, *J. R. R. Tolkien*, p. 97.

'the inmost province of the fading isle [...]' and 'The holy fairies and immortal elves [...]': J. R. R. Tolkien, *The Book of Lost Tales: Part I*, ed. Christopher Tolkien, The History of Middle-earth 1 (London: George Allen and Unwin, 1983), p. 34.

'not any common Earth [...]' and 'Merlin's Isle of Gramarye': Rudyard Kipling, *Puck of Pook's Hill and Rewards and Fairies*, ed. Donald Mackenzie (Oxford: Oxford University Press, 1993), p. 6.

'I saw them come [...]': Kipling, *Puck of Pook's Hill and Rewards and Fairies*, pp. 10–11.

'Ingolondë the fair and sorrowful': Tolkien, *The Shaping of Middle-earth*, p. 108.

'In the tales of J. R. R. Tolkien [...]': R. W. Burchfield (ed.), *A Supplement to the Oxford English Dictionary* (Oxford: Oxford University Press, 1976), p. 111.

'dudmen, hell-hounds, dopple-gangers [...]': James Hardy (ed.), *The Denham Tracts: A Collection of Folklore by Michael Aislabie*

Denham, 2 vols, Publications of the Folklore Society 29, 35 (London: Folklore Society, 1892–5), II, 79.

'I suppose hobbits need some description [...]': Tolkien, *The Hobbit*, pp. 11–12.

'There is little or no magic about them [...]': Tolkien, *The Hobbit*, p. 12.

'Hobbits are an unobtrusive but very ancient people [...]': Tolkien, *The Lord of the Rings*, p. 1.

'only a little people [...]': Tolkien, *The Lord of the Rings*, p. 434.

'folk of legend': Tolkien, *The Lord of the Rings*, p. 557.

'not the first halfling [...]': Tolkien, *The Lord of the Rings*, p. 811.

'You should never have gone [...]': Tolkien, *The Lord of the Rings*, p. 94.

'He spoke funny': Tolkien, *The Lord of the Rings*, p. 76.

'Ease and peace [...]', 'difficult to daunt', 'doughty at bay', and 'survive rough handling [...]': Tolkien, *The Lord of the Rings*, p. 6.

'no listener would have guessed [...]': Tolkien, *The Lord of the Rings*, p. 458.

'suddenly the slow-kindled courage [...]': Tolkien, *The Lord of the Rings*, p. 841.

'this is the hour of the Shire-folk': Tolkien, *The Lord of the Rings*, p. 270.

'at about the latitude of Oxford': Tolkien, *Letters*, p. 376 (no. 294).

'Little Englander': Anna Vaninskaya, 'Periodizing Tolkien: The Romantic Modern', in Stuart D. Lee (ed.), *A Companion to J. R. R. Tolkien*, rev. ed. (Chichester: Wiley Blackwell, 2022), pp. 337–51, at pp. 343–8.

Chapter 5: Language

'Great became their knowledge [...]': Tolkien, *The Silmarillion*, p. 60.

'the Noldor were of all the Eldar [...]', 'individual pleasure in the sounds and forms of words', and 'this *lámatyávë* was held a mark of individuality [...]': Tolkien, *Morgoth's Ring*, p. 215.

'shown not so much in the acquisition of new tongues [...]': J. R. R. Tolkien, *The War of the Jewels. The Later Silmarillion, Part Two: The Legends of Beleriand*, ed. Christopher Tolkien, The History of Middle-earth 11 (London: HarperCollins, 1994), p. 413.

'given perhaps more pleasure [...]': Tolkien, *The Monsters and the Critics*, p. 197 n. 33.

'most English-speaking people [...]': Tolkien, *The Monsters and the Critics*, p. 190.

'*cellar doors* are extraordinarily frequent': Tolkien, *The Monsters and the Critics*, pp. 190–1.

'the nature of this *pleasure* […]' and '[make] more precise some of the features of style […]': Tolkien, *The Monsters and the Critics*, p. 191.

'felt most strongly […]': Tolkien, *The Monsters and the Critics*, p. 190.

'a great freshness of perception […]': Tolkien, *The Monsters and the Critics*, p. 206.

'personally most interested perhaps in word-form […]': Tolkien, *The Monsters and the Critics*, p. 211.

'I liked its word-style […]': Tolkien, *Sauron Defeated*, p. 235.

'beautiful, in its simple and euphonious style': Tolkien, *Sauron Defeated*, p. 241.

'an excess of euphony': J. R. R. Tolkien, *The Story of Kullervo*, ed. Verlyn Flieger (London: HarperCollins, 2010), pp. 77, 115.

'the dreadful language of the Wargs' and 'it sounded terrible to him […]: Tolkien, *The Hobbit*, p. 91.

'hideous': Tolkien, *The Lord of the Rings*, p. 327.

'their abominable tongue' and '*Uglúk u bagronk sha pushdug* […]': Tolkien, *The Lord of the Rings*, p. 445.

'it is difficult to fit meaning […]': Tolkien, *Sauron Defeated*, p. 239.

'language-building' and 'code-making': Tolkien, *Sauron Defeated*, p. 240.

Elrohir and Elladan: Tolkien, *Letters*, p. 282 (no. 211).

Essecilmë or 'Name-choosing': Tolkien, *Morgoth's Ring*, p. 214.

'names of insight' or 'foresight' and 'might give a name to her child […]': Tolkien, *Morgoth's Ring*, p. 216.

'in boyhood […]': Tolkien, *The War of the Jewels*, p. 337.

Eärendil or Earendel: J. R. R. Tolkien, *The Peoples of Middle-earth*, ed. Christopher Tolkien, The History of Middle-earth 12 (London: HarperCollins, 1996), p. 348.

'Elves love the making of words […]': J. R. R. Tolkien, *The Lost Road and Other Writings: Language and Legend before 'The Lord of the Rings'*, ed. Christopher Tolkien, The History of Middle-earth 5 (London: Unwin Hyman, 1987), p. 168.

'became early fixed […]': Tolkien, *The Lost Road*, p. 172.

'growth and change were swift for all living things': Tolkien, *The Lost Road*, p. 177.

AM- and NAR-: Tolkien, *The Lost Road*, pp. 348, 374.

KW- and TH-: Tolkien, *The Lost Road*, pp. 366, 392.

'would indeed do a story in Elvish […]': Clyde S. Kilby, *Tolkien and the Silmarillion* (Wheaton: Harold Shaw, 1976), p. 33.

'Ae Adar nín i vi Menel [...]': J. R. R. Tolkien, '*Ae Adar Nín*: The Lord's Prayer in Sindarin', ed. Bill Welden, *Vinyar Tengwar* 44 (2002), 21–30.

'*a-lalla-lalla-rumba-kamanda-lindor-burúmë*': Tolkien, *The Lord of the Rings*, p. 465.

'much of the talk was intelligible[...]' and 'apparently the members [...]': Tolkien, *The Lord of the Rings*, p. 445.

'surprise' and 'spoke the Common Speech [...]': Tolkien, *The Lord of the Rings*, p. 832.

'the Common Language, speaking slowly': Tolkien, *The Lord of the Rings*, p. 343.

'sing[s] softly to himself in his own tongue': Tolkien, *The Lord of the Rings*, p. 429.

'using the Common Speech of the West': Tolkien, *The Lord of the Rings*, p. 432.

'humming in Entish or Elvish [...]': Tolkien, *The Lord of the Rings*, p. 478.

'fragments of Elf-speech strung together [...]': Tolkien, *The Lord of the Rings*, p. 1131.

'go[ne] abroad for the gathering of news' and 'speak little': Tolkien, *The Lord of the Rings*, p. 343.

'now in the elven-tongue [...]': Tolkien, *The Lord of the Rings*, p. 954.

'written in the tongues of Men and Dwarves': Tolkien, *The Lord of the Rings*, p. 320.

'carved in the tongues of Gondor and the Mark': Tolkien, *The Lord of the Rings*, p. 845.

'*Aiya Eärendil Elenion Ancalima!*' and 'knew not what he had spoken': Tolkien, *The Lord of the Rings*, p. 720.

'his tongue was loosed [...]' and '*A Elbereth Gilthoniel*': Tolkien, *The Lord of the Rings*, p. 729.

'liked runes and letters [...]': Tolkien, *The Hobbit*, p. 52.

'the Noldor first bethought them [...]': Tolkien, *The Silmarillion*, p. 63.

'sitting in his study [...]' and 'There and Back Again, a Hobbit's Holiday': Tolkien, *The Hobbit*, p. 254.

'the record of a year's journey [...]': Tolkien, *The Hobbit*, title-page.

'The Downfall of the Lord of the Rings [...]': Tolkien, *The Lord of the Rings*, p. 1027.

'[Frodo's] limited acquaintance with Sindarin' and 'misled': Tolkien, *The Lord of the Rings*, p. 1127 n. 1.

'translated from the Red Book of Westmarch [...]': Tolkien, *The Lord of the Rings*, title-page.

'in presenting the matter of the Red Book [...]', 'languages alien to the Common Speech [...]', and 'the Common Speech, as the language of the Hobbits [...]': Tolkien, *The Lord of the Rings*, p. 1133.

'translated all Westron names [...]': Tolkien, *The Lord of the Rings*, p. 1134.

Chapter 6: Sources

'New-old': Christopher Ricks (ed.), *Tennyson: A Selected Edition*, rev. ed. (Harlow: Pearson Longman, 2007), p. 974.

'no songs had alluded to him [...]': Tolkien, *The Hobbit*, p. 170.

'knights' and 'warriors': Tolkien, *The Monsters and the Critics*, p. 57.

'relatively advanced and artistic' and 'crude and semi-barbaric Normans': J. R. R. Tolkien, *The Battle of Maldon, together with The Homecoming of Beorhtnoth Beorhthelm's Son and 'The Tradition of Versification in Old English'*, ed. Peter Grybauskas (London: HarperCollins, 2023), p. 87.

'modern thirst [...]' and 'prob[ably] unwholesome': Tolkien, *The Story of Kullervo*, p. 76.

'inspired by reading *Pearl* for examination purposes' and 'where ageless afternoon goes by [...]': Tolkien, *The Lost Road*, p. 98.

'no blemish or sickness [...]': Tolkien, *The Lord of the Rings*, pp. 350–1.

'dark cavernous opening in a great cliff-wall': Tolkien, *The Hobbit*, p. 175.

'a stone-arch standing [...]': J. R. R. Tolkien, *Beowulf: A Translation and Commentary*, ed. Christopher Tolkien (London: HarperCollins, 2014), p. 87.

'most like to flame': Tolkien, *Beowulf*, p. 33.

'burned with a pale flame': Tolkien, *The Hobbit*, p. 76.

'claws of steel': Tolkien, *The Book of Lost Tales: Part II*, pp. 169, 179.

'a dark form, of man-shape maybe [...]': Tolkien, *The Lord of the Rings*, p. 329.

'of these was one [...]': Tolkien, *Beowulf*, p. 52.

Ilúvatar as 'All-Father': Tolkien, *The War of the Jewels*, p. 402.

'the greatest of the forests [...]': Tolkien, *The Hobbit*, p. 119.

'I am afraid trolls really do behave [...]': Tolkien, *The Hobbit*, p. 37.

'knew, of course, that the riddle-game was sacred [...]': Tolkien, *The Hobbit*, p. 74.

'discussing dragon-slayings [...]': Tolkien, *The Hobbit*, p. 195.

'I am Ringwinner and Luckwearer [...]' and 'This of course is the way to talk [...]': Tolkien, *The Hobbit*, pp. 190–1.

'goblin fighters [...] sitting on drasils': J. R. R. Tolkien, *Letters from Father Christmas*, ed. Baillie Tolkien, rev. ed. (London: HarperCollins, 2009), p. 89.

'wrote a short treatise [...]': Tolkien, *The Lord of the Rings*, p. 15.

'lo, an ill reek ariseth yonder': Tolkien, *The Story of Kullervo*, p. 6.

'Mount Doom was burning [...]': Tolkien, *The Lord of the Rings*, p. 401.

'the reeking towers of Thangorodrim': Tolkien, *Morgoth's Ring*, p. 109.

'Théoden King': Tolkien, *The Lord of the Rings*, pp. 540, 845 (for example).

'fair words and true': Tolkien, *The Hobbit*, p. 223.

'grim men and bad': Tolkien, *The Hobbit*, p. 248.

'Thorin Thrain's son Oakenshield': Tolkien, *The Hobbit*, p. 224.

'indispensable': Tolkien, *Letters*, p. 11 (no. 6).

'the greatest and most convincing writer [...]': Tolkien, *Letters*, p. 258 (no. 199).

'Whilom, as tells the tale [...]': William Morris, *The Water of the Wondrous Isles* (London: Longmans, Green and Co., 1897), p. 1.

'Giants they seemed to [Frodo]', 'Upon great pedestals [...]', and 'Great power and majesty [...]': Tolkien, *The Lord of the Rings*, p. 392.

'Wild Wood': John D. Rateliff, *The History of The Hobbit. Part One: Mr Baggins* (London: HarperCollins, 2007), frontispiece.

'lie near the borders of Faërie': Tolkien, *The Monsters and the Critics*, p. 117.

Pilgrimage to the Lake District: C. S. Lewis, *Collected Letters: Volume II Books, Broadcasts, and the War, 1931–1949*, ed. Walter Hooper (London: HarperCollins, 2004), pp. 537–8.

'little buzzflies with butterfly wings [...]' and 'made-up things': Kipling, *Puck of Pook's Hill and Rewards and Fairies*, p. 13.

'a small, brown, broad-shouldered, pointy-eared person [...]', 'no taller', and 'bare, hairy feet': Kipling, *Puck of Pook's Hill and Rewards and Fairies*, p. 8.

'the spirit of the (vanishing) Oxford and Berkshire countryside': Tolkien, *Letters*, p. 26 (no. 19).

'oldest Old Thing in England': Kipling, *Puck of Pook's Hill and Rewards and Fairies*, p. 9.

'older than the old': Tolkien, *The Lord of the Rings*, p. 265.

'the oldest living thing [...]': Tolkien, *The Lord of the Rings*, p. 500.

'unconscious source-book': Tolkien, *Letters*, p. 215 (no. 163).

'as though it had fallen from the sky': Tolkien, *The Lord of the Rings*, p. 789.

'Can you better it?' and 'Maybe, I could [...]': Tolkien, *The Lord of the Rings*, p. 489.

'all things were made for [men's] service': J. R. R. Tolkien, *Unfinished Tales of Númenor and Middle-earth*, ed. Christopher Tolkien (London: George Allen and Unwin, 1980), p. 207.

'not made for perilous quests': Tolkien, *The Lord of the Rings*, p. 61.

Chapter 7: Middle-earth

'so great was the fury [...]': Tolkien, *The Silmarillion*, p. 252.

'Straight Road': Tolkien, *The Silmarillion*, p. 286.

'Atalantë in the Eldarin tongue': Tolkien, *The Silmarillion*, p. 281.

'went into the east of Middle-earth [...]': Tolkien, *The Silmarillion*, p. 300.

'these legends are North-centred': Tolkien, *Unfinished Tales*, p. 398.

'crossed many mountains and many rivers [...]': Tolkien, *The Lord of the Rings*, p. 248.

'loved maps [...]': Tolkien, *The Hobbit*, p. 26.

'admits us to a world of its own [...]': Lewis, *Image and Imagination*, p. 95.

W. H. Auden and pets: Catherine McIlwaine, *Tolkien: Maker of Middle-earth* (Oxford: Bodleian Library, 2018), p. 93.

'they went down the slope [...]': Tolkien, *The Lord of the Rings*, p. 73.

'The woods on either side became denser [...]': Tolkien, *The Lord of the Rings*, p. 81.

Anfractuosity: C. S. Lewis, *The Problem of Pain* (London: Geoffrey Bles, 1940), p. 13.

'the wonder of the neighbourhood' and 'one of the finest in the world': Tolkien, *The Lord of the Rings*, p. 1023.

'Nobody cares for the woods [...]': Tolkien, *The Lord of the Rings*, p. 472.

'long ago in the quiet of the world [...]': Tolkien, *The Hobbit*, p. 13.

'the one small garden of a free gardener': Tolkien, *The Lord of the Rings*, p. 901.

'the lover of all things that grow [...]': Tolkien, *The Silmarillion*, p. 27.

'the seeds that Yavanna had sown [...]': Tolkien, *The Silmarillion*, p. 35.

'All my works are dear to me [...]': Tolkien, *The Silmarillion*, p. 45.

'it is not unlikely that they invented [...]': Tolkien, *The Hobbit*, p. 60.

'sweet grass' and 'bruised and blackened': Tolkien, *The Lord of the Rings*, p. 424.

'does not care for growing things' and 'a mind of metal and wheels': Tolkien, *The Lord of the Rings*, p. 473.

'slaves and machines': Tolkien, *The Lord of the Rings*, p. 567.

'Iron wheels revolved there endlessly [...]': Tolkien, *The Lord of the Rings*, pp. 554–5.

'this was [their] own country [...]', 'tall chimney of brick', and 'pouring out black smoke [...]': Tolkien, *The Lord of the Rings*, p. 1004.

'worse than Mordor' and 'Yes, this is Mordor [...]': Tolkien, *The Lord of the Rings*, p. 1018.

'Spring surpassed [Sam's] wildest hopes', 'wonderful sunshine and delicious rain', and 'air of richness and growth': Tolkien, *The Lord of the Rings*, p. 1023.

'the wholly pernicious and unscientific race-doctrine': Tolkien, *Letters*, p. 37 (no. 29).

'language is the prime differentiator of peoples [...]': Tolkien, *The Monsters and the Critics*, p. 166.

'breeds' of Hobbits: Tolkien, *The Lord of the Rings*, p. 3.

Appearance of Orcs: Tolkien, *The Lord of the Rings*, pp. 325, 451 (for example).

'even in Bilbo's time [...]': Tolkien, *The Lord of the Rings*, pp. 3–4.

'the blood of Westernesse [...]': Tolkien, *The Lord of the Rings*, p. 759.

'occult entity like a racial temperament [...]': R. G. Collingwood, *An Autobiography* (Oxford: Oxford University Press, 1939), pp. 142–3.

'modern myth', 'fixed not only in shape', and 'endowed even in the mists of antiquity [...]': Tolkien, *The Monsters and the Critics*, p. 171.

'The wide world is all about you [...]': Tolkien, *The Lord of the Rings*, p. 83.

'Outsiders': Tolkien, *The Lord of the Rings*, pp. 150, 154.

'I do not feel too sure [...]': Tolkien, *The Lord of the Rings*, p. 358.

'these elves and half-elves and wizards': Tolkien, *The Lord of the Rings*, p. 398.

'wondered what the man's name was [...]': Tolkien, *The Lord of the Rings*, p. 661.

'it seemed to him that he looked [...]': Tolkien, *The Lord of the Rings*, p. 356.

'looking for lands [...]': Tolkien, *The Lord of the Rings*, p. 155.

'My political opinions [...]': Tolkien, *Letters*, p. 63 (no. 52).

'The King pardoned the Easterlings [...]': Tolkien, *The Lord of the Rings*, p. 968.

'Aragorn gave to Faramir [...]': Tolkien, *The Lord of the Rings*, p. 969.

'The Forest of Drúadan he [gave] to Ghân-buri-Ghân [...]': Tolkien, *The Lord of the Rings*, p. 976.

'will give to Ents all this valley [...]': Tolkien, *The Lord of the Rings*, p. 980.

'let Bree alone': Tolkien, *The Lord of the Rings*, p. 994.

'King Elessar issues an edict [...]': Tolkien, *The Lord of the Rings*, p. 1097.

'for her memory, her ancientry, her beauty [...]' and 'feared': Tolkien, *The Lord of the Rings*, p. 672.

'those days, now long ago [...]' and 'villages were proud and independent still': J. R. R. Tolkien, *Farmer Giles of Ham* (London: George Allen and Unwin, 1949), p. 9.

'the noise of marching feet': Tolkien, *The Lord of the Rings*, p. 930.

'hardly any 'government'', 'families for the most part [...]', and 'generous and not greedy [...]': Tolkien, *The Lord of the Rings*, p. 9.

'like minding other folk's business [...]': Tolkien, *The Lord of the Rings*, p. 1002.

'list of Rules': Tolkien, *The Lord of the Rings*, p. 1000.

'laws of free will [...]': Tolkien, *The Lord of the Rings*, p. 9.

'If I hear *not allowed* [...]': Tolkien, *The Lord of the Rings*, p. 1002.

'a type of Christian quasi-anarchist [...]': Brian Rosebury, *Tolkien: A Cultural Phenomenon* (Basingstoke: Palgrave Macmillan, 2003), p. 179.

'the most improper job [...]' and 'not one in a million [...]': Tolkien, *Letters*, p. 64 (no. 52).

Chapter 8: Elegy

'heroic-elegiac': Tolkien, *The Monsters and the Critics*, p. 31.

'the desire to express [his] *feeling* [...]': Tolkien, *Letters*, p. 78 (no. 66).

'he seemed to have grown almost to giant-size [...]': Tolkien, *The Hobbit*, p. 244.

'Victory after all, I suppose! [...]': Tolkien, *The Hobbit*, p. 242.

'needlessly noble' and 'to give minstrels matter [...]': Tolkien, *The Battle of Maldon*, p. 20.

'The tremendous things that happened afterwards [...]': Tolkien, *The Hobbit*, p. 184.

'they checked their steeds [...]': Tolkien, *The Lord of the Rings*, p. 431.

'pocked with great holes [...]': Tolkien, *The Lord of the Rings*, p. 934.

'it need not have happened [...]' and 'so do all [...]': Tolkien, *The Lord of the Rings*, p. 51.

'the great storm is coming [...]': Tolkien, *The Lord of the Rings*, p. 495.

'everywhere he looked [...]': Tolkien, *The Lord of the Rings*, p. 400.

'Help me, Pippin! [...]': Tolkien, *The Lord of the Rings*, p. 859.

'wounds that cannot be wholly cured', 'the wound aches [...]', and 'no real going back': Tolkien, *The Lord of the Rings*, p. 989.

'Pippin looked ruefully [...]': Tolkien, *The Lord of the Rings*, p. 806.

'kindle no more lights [...]': Tolkien, *The Lord of the Rings*, p. 793.

'the heart-racking sense [...]': Tolkien, *Letters*, p. 110 (no. 96).

'glimpses of a large history [...]' and 'unattainable vistas': Tolkien, *Letters*, p. 333 (no. 247).

'a dark antiquity of sorrow': Tolkien, *The Monsters and the Critics*, p. 27.

'the ruined walls and paving-stones [...]': Tolkien, *The Lord of the Rings*, p. 300.

'the dwindling ruins of a road [...]': Tolkien, *The Lord of the Rings*, p. 396.

'made in a long lost time' and 'all signs of stonework [...]': Tolkien, *The Lord of the Rings*, p. 649.

'the coming of death without wound' and 'the short span [...]': Tolkien, *The War of the Jewels*, p. 52.

'No heart of Man is content [...]': Tolkien, *Morgoth's Ring*, p. 307.

'Death is an uttermost end [...]': Tolkien, *Morgoth's Ring*, p. 311.

'It is one with this gift of freedom [...]': Tolkien, *Morgoth's Ring*, p. 37.

'willed that the hearts of Men [...]': Tolkien, *Morgoth's Ring*, p. 36.

'these lands of exile': Tolkien, *The Lord of the Rings*, p. 378.

'the sigh and murmur of the sea [...]': Tolkien, *Sauron Defeated*, p. 119.

'fallen man' and 'this fallen world': Tolkien, *Letters*, pp. 48–52, 98 (nos 43, 87) (for example).

'blended with an immeasurable sorrow': Tolkien, *Morgoth's Ring*, p. 10.

'all things, save in Aman [...]': Tolkien, *Morgoth's Ring*, p. 255.

'a darkness lies behind us': Tolkien, *The Silmarillion*, p. 141.

'some of [them] hid themselves': Tolkien, *Morgoth's Ring*, p. 73.

'the fall of the most gifted kindred [...]' and 'exile from Valinor':
    Tolkien, *Letters*, p. 148 (no. 131).
'I have failed' and 'It is I that have failed': Tolkien, *The Lord of the Rings*, p. 414.
'Where shall I find courage?': Tolkien, *The Lord of the Rings*, p. 84.
'Why, cousin, one of them went [...]': Tolkien, *The Lord of the Rings*, p. 966.
'I am afraid [...]': Tolkien, *The Lord of the Rings*, p. 398.
'Now it's come to the point [...]': Tolkien, *The Lord of the Rings*, p. 403.
'I am weary [...]': Tolkien, *The Lord of the Rings*, p. 668.
'I am tired [...]': Tolkien, *The Lord of the Rings*, p. 918.
'the last foundation of *Estel* [...]' and 'part of our wound [...]':
    Tolkien, *Morgoth's Ring*, p. 320.
'small but indomitable': Tolkien, *The Lord of the Rings*, p. 938.
'their wills did not yield [...]' and 'knew all the arguments [...]':
    Tolkien, *The Lord of the Rings*, p. 940.
'I do not choose now to do [...]': Tolkien, *The Lord of the Rings*, p. 945.
'if you re-read all the passages [...]': Tolkien, *Letters*, p. 251 (no. 191).
'a sad story': Tolkien, *The Lord of the Rings*, p. 54.
'wholly ruined' and 'hated it and loved it [...]': Tolkien, *The Lord of the Rings*, p. 55.
'pity', 'it was Pity that stayed his hand', 'not much hope [...]', and 'there
    is a chance of it': Tolkien, *The Lord of the Rings*, p. 59.
'For now that I see him [...]': Tolkien, *The Lord of the Rings*, p. 615.
'Frodo tamed Gollum [...]': J. R. R. Tolkien, *The Return of the King,
    being the third part of The Lord of the Rings* (London: George
    Allen and Unwin, 1955), p. 12.
'Gollum fell back into evil': Tolkien, *The Return of the King*, p. 13.
'Slowly putting out a trembling hand [...]': Tolkien, *The Lord of the Rings*, p. 714.
'sneak': Tolkien, *The Lord of the Rings*, p. 715.
'strike this thing lying in the dust [...]': Tolkien, *The Lord of the Rings*, p. 944.
'his chief part had been [...]': Tolkien, *The Lord of the Rings*, p. 1016.
'save' Lotho: Tolkien, *The Lord of the Rings*, p. 1006.
'He is fallen [...]': Tolkien, *The Lord of the Rings*, p. 1019.
'The consolation of fairy-stories [...]': Tolkien, *The Monsters and the Critics*, p. 153.

'the greatest and most complete [...]': Tolkien, *The Monsters and the Critics*, p. 156.

'a happiness that brings tears [...]': Tolkien, *Sauron Defeated*, p. 190.

'Sing and rejoice [...]': Tolkien, *The Lord of the Rings*, p. 963.

'Is everything sad going to come untrue?': Tolkien, *The Lord of the Rings*, p. 951.

The Lord of the Rings as fundamentally Christian: Tolkien, *Letters*, p. 172 (no. 142).

'private day-dreaming': J. R. R. Tolkien, *Tree and Leaf* (London: George Allen and Unwin, 1964), p. 91.

'He gazed at the Tree [...]': Tolkien, *Tree and Leaf*, p. 85.

'very useful indeed [...]' and 'it works wonders': Tolkien, *Tree and Leaf*, p. 92.

'Nothing has astonished me more [...]': Tolkien, *Letters*, p. 221 (no. 165).

'it remains an unfailing delight [...]': Tolkien, *Letters*, p. 209 (no. 159).

Bibliography

Major works by J. R. R. Tolkien

A Middle English Vocabulary (Oxford: Clarendon Press, 1922).

With E. V. Gordon (eds), *Sir Gawain and the Green Knight* (Oxford: Clarendon Press, 1925).

The Hobbit, or There and Back Again (London: George Allen and Unwin, 1937).

Farmer Giles of Ham (London: George Allen and Unwin, 1949).

The Fellowship of the Ring, being the first part of The Lord of the Rings (London: George Allen and Unwin, 1954).

The Two Towers, being the second part of The Lord of the Rings (London: George Allen and Unwin, 1954).

The Return of the King, being the third part of The Lord of the Rings (London: George Allen and Unwin, 1955).

The Adventures of Tom Bombadil (London: George Allen and Unwin, 1962).

(Ed.), *Ancrene Wisse: The English Text of the Ancrene Riwle, edited from MS Corpus Christi College Cambridge 402*, Early English Text Society Original Series 249 (Oxford: Early English Text Society, 1962).

Tree and Leaf (London: George Allen and Unwin, 1964).

Smith of Wootton Major (London: George Allen and Unwin, 1967).

With Donald Swann, *The Road Goes Ever On: A Song Cycle* (London: George Allen and Unwin, 1968).

Sir Gawain and the Green Knight, Pearl, and Sir Orfeo, ed. Christopher Tolkien (London: George Allen and Unwin, 1975).

The Father Christmas Letters, ed. Baillie Tolkien (London: George
  Allen and Unwin, 1976).

The Silmarillion, ed. Christopher Tolkien (London: George Allen and
  Unwin, 1977).

Unfinished Tales of Númenor and Middle-earth, ed. Christopher
  Tolkien (London: George Allen and Unwin, 1980).

Letters, ed. Humphrey Carpenter with Christopher Tolkien (London:
  George Allen and Unwin, 1981).

The Old English Exodus: Text, Translation, and Commentary, ed.
  Joan Turville-Petre (Oxford: Clarendon Press, 1981).

Finn and Hengest: The Fragment and the Episode, ed. Alan Bliss
  (London: George Allen and Unwin, 1982).

Mr Bliss (London: George Allen and Unwin, 1982).

The Monsters and the Critics and Other Essays, ed. Christopher
  Tolkien (London: George Allen and Unwin, 1983).

The Book of Lost Tales: Part I, ed. Christopher Tolkien, The History of
  Middle-earth 1 (London: George Allen and Unwin, 1983).

The Book of Lost Tales: Part II, ed. Christopher Tolkien, The History of
  Middle-earth 2 (London: George Allen and Unwin, 1984).

The Lays of Beleriand, ed. Christopher Tolkien, The History of
  Middle-earth 3 (London: George Allen and Unwin, 1985).

*The Shaping of Middle-earth: The Quenta, the Ambarkanta, and the
  Annals, together with the earliest 'Silmarillion' and the first Map*,
  ed. Christopher Tolkien, The History of Middle-earth 4 (London:
  George Allen and Unwin, 1986).

*The Lost Road and Other Writings: Language and Legend before 'The
  Lord of the Rings'*, ed. Christopher Tolkien, The History of
  Middle-earth 5 (London: Unwin Hyman, 1987).

*The Return of the Shadow: The History of The Lord of the Rings, Part
  One*, ed. Christopher Tolkien, The History of Middle-earth 6
  (London: Unwin Hyman, 1988).

*The Treason of Isengard: The History of The Lord of the Rings, Part
  Two*, ed. Christopher Tolkien, The History of Middle-earth 7
  (London: Unwin Hyman, 1989).

The War of the Ring: The History of The Lord of the Rings, Part Three,
  ed. Christopher Tolkien, The History of Middle-earth 8 (London:
  Unwin Hyman, 1990).

*Sauron Defeated: The End of the Third Age. The History of the Lord of
  the Rings, Part Four*, ed. Christopher Tolkien, The History of
  Middle-earth 9 (London: HarperCollins, 1992).

Morgoth's Ring. The Later Silmarillion, Part One: The Legends of Aman, ed. Christopher Tolkien, The History of Middle-earth 10 (London: HarperCollins, 1993).

The War of the Jewels. The Later Silmarillion, Part Two: The Legends of Beleriand, ed. Christopher Tolkien, The History of Middle-earth 11 (London: HarperCollins, 1994).

The Peoples of Middle-earth, ed. Christopher Tolkien, The History of Middle-earth 12 (London: HarperCollins, 1996).

Roverandom, ed. Christina Scull and Wayne G. Hammond (London: HarperCollins, 1998).

Beowulf and the Critics, ed. Michael D. C. Drout (Tempe, AZ: Arizona Center for Medieval and Renaissance Studies, 2002).

The Children of Húrin, ed. Christopher Tolkien (London: HarperCollins, 2007).

The History of the Hobbit, ed. John D. Rateliff, 2 vols (London: HarperCollins, 2007).

On Fairy-Stories: Expanded Edition, with Commentary and Notes, ed. Verlyn Flieger and Douglas A. Anderson (London: HarperCollins, 2008).

The Legend of Sigurd and Gudrún, ed. Christopher Tolkien (London: HarperCollins, 2009).

The Story of Kullervo, ed. Verlyn Flieger (London: HarperCollins, 2010).

The Fall of Arthur, ed. Christopher Tolkien (London: HarperCollins, 2013).

Beowulf: A Translation and Commentary, ed. Christopher Tolkien (London: HarperCollins, 2014).

The Lay of Aotrou and Itroun, together with the Corrigan Poems, ed. Verlyn Flieger (London: HarperCollins, 2016).

A Secret Vice: Tolkien on Invented Languages, ed. Dimitra Fimi and Andrew Higgins (London: HarperCollins, 2016).

The Fall of Gondolin, ed. Christopher Tolkien (London: HarperCollins, 2018).

The Nature of Middle-earth: Late Writings on the Lands, Inhabitants, and Metaphysics of Middle-earth, ed. Carl F. Hostetter (London: HarperCollins, 2021).

The Battle of Maldon, together with The Homecoming of Beorhtnoth Beorhthelm's Son and 'The Tradition of Versification in Old English', ed. Peter Grybauskas (London: HarperCollins, 2023).

Further reading

With a few exceptions, this list is confined to book-length works, rather than articles or collections of essays. Early scholarship on Tolkien focused especially on his relation to his medieval sources and his position in the evolution of fantasy literature. More recent topics to gain prominence have included his status as a writer shaped by the experience of the First World War, his position as a Christian (and specifically Catholic) author, and his pertinence to contemporary debates about culture and identity.

Biography and reference

Humphrey Carpenter, *J. R. R. Tolkien: A Biography* (London: George Allen and Unwin, 1977).

Humphrey Carpenter, *The Inklings: C. S. Lewis, J. R. R. Tolkien, Charles Williams and Their Friends* (London: George Allen and Unwin, 1978).

Michael D. C. Drout (ed.), *J. R. R. Tolkien Encyclopedia: Scholarship and Critical Assessment* (London: Routledge, 2007).

Raymond Edwards, *Tolkien* (Marlborough: Robert Hale, 2014).

John Garth, *Tolkien and the Great War: The Threshold of Middle-earth* (London: HarperCollins, 2003).

John Garth, *The Worlds of J. R. R. Tolkien: The Places that Inspired Middle-earth* (London: Frances Lincoln, 2020).

Diana Pavlac Glyer, *The Company They Keep: C. S. Lewis and J. R. R. Tolkien as Writers in Community* (Kent, OH: Kent State University Press, 2007).

Wayne G. Hammond, *J. R. R. Tolkien: A Descriptive Bibliography* (New Castle, DE: Oak Knoll, 1993).

Catherine McIlwaine, *Tolkien: Maker of Middle-earth* (Oxford: Bodleian Library, 2018).

Christina Scull and Wayne G. Hammond, *The J. R. R. Tolkien Companion and Guide*, rev. ed., 3 vols (London: HarperCollins, 2017).

Scholarship and medievalism

Mark Atherton, *There and Back Again: J. R. R. Tolkien and the Origins of The Hobbit* (London: Tauris, 2012).

John M. Bowers, *Tolkien's Lost Chaucer* (Oxford: Oxford University Press, 2019).

Marjorie Burns, *Perilous Realms: Celtic and Norse in Tolkien's Middle-earth* (Toronto: University of Toronto Press, 2005).

Peter Gilliver, Jeremy Marshall, and Edmund Weiner, *The Ring of Words: Tolkien and the Oxford English Dictionary* (Oxford: Oxford University Press, 2006).

Stuart D. Lee and Elizabeth Solopova, *The Keys of Middle-earth: Discovering Medieval Literature through the Fiction of J. R. R. Tolkien* (Basingstoke: Palgrave Macmillan, 2005).

Carl Phelpstead, *Tolkien and Wales: Language, Literature and Identity* (Cardiff: University of Wales Press, 2011).

Tom Shippey, *The Road to Middle-earth*, rev. ed. (London: HarperCollins, 2005).

Literary and intellectual contexts

Michael Alexander, *Medievalism: The Middle Ages in Modern England* (New Haven: Yale University Press, 2007).

Maria Sachiko Cecire, *Re-enchanted: The Rise of Children's Fantasy Literature in the Twentieth Century* (Minneapolis: University of Minnesota Press, 2019).

Oronzo Cilli, *Tolkien's Library: An Annotated Checklist* (Edinburgh: Luna Press, 2019).

Dimitra Fimi, *Tolkien, Race and Cultural History: From Fairies to Hobbits* (Basingstoke: Palgrave Macmillan, 2010).

Jason Fisher (ed.), *Tolkien and the Study of His Sources: Critical Essays* (Jefferson, NC: McFarland and Co., 2011).

Jared Lobdell, *The Rise of Tolkienian Fantasy* (Chicago: Open Court, 2005).

Holly Ordway, *Tolkien's Modern Reading: Middle-earth beyond the Middle Ages* (Park Ridge: Word on Fire, 2021).

Diane Purkiss, *Troublesome Things: A History of Fairies and Fairy Stories* (London: Allen Lane, 2000).

Michael Saler, *As If: Modern Enchantment and the Literary Prehistory of Virtual Reality* (New York: Oxford University Press, 2012).

Carole G. Silver, *Strange and Secret Peoples: Fairies and Victorian Consciousness* (New York: Oxford University Press, 1999).

Marina Warner, *Fairy Tale: A Very Short Introduction* (Oxford: Oxford University Press, 2018).

Jamie Williamson, *The Evolution of Modern Fantasy: From Antiquarianism to the Ballantine Adult Fantasy Series* (Basingstoke: Palgrave Macmillan, 2015).

Criticism and interpretation

Douglas A. Anderson (ed.), *The Annotated Hobbit*, rev. ed. (London: HarperCollins, 2003).

Stratford Caldecott, *The Power of the Ring: The Spiritual Vision behind The Hobbit and The Lord of the Rings*, rev. ed. (New York: Crossroad Publishing, 2012).

Jane Chance, *Tolkien's Art: A Mythology for England*, rev. ed. (Lexington: University Press of Kentucky, 2001).

Jane Chance, *Tolkien, Self and Other: 'This Queer Creature'* (Basingstoke: Palgrave Macmillan, 2016).

Patrick Curry, *Defending Middle-earth. Tolkien: Myth and Modernity* (London: HarperCollins, 1998).

Verlyn Flieger, *Splintered Light: Logos and Language in Tolkien's World*, rev. ed. (Kent, OH: Kent State University Press, 2002).

Verlyn Flieger, *Interrupted Music: The Making of Tolkien's Mythology* (Kent, OH: Kent State University Press, 2005).

Verlyn Flieger and Carl F. Hostetter (eds), *Tolkien's Legendarium: Essays on the History of Middle-earth* (Westport, CT: Greenwood Press, 2000).

Nick Groom, *Twenty-First-Century Tolkien: What Middle-Earth Means to Us Today* (London: Atlantic, 2022).

Wayne G. Hammond and Christina Scull, *J. R. R. Tolkien, Artist and Illustrator* (London: HarperCollins, 1995).

Wayne G. Hammond and Christina Scull, *The Lord of the Rings: A Reader's Companion* (London: HarperCollins, 2005).

Paul H. Kocher, *Master of Middle-earth: The Achievement of J. R. R. Tolkien* (London: Thames and Hudson, 1972).

Stuart D. Lee (ed.), *A Companion to J. R. R. Tolkien*, rev. ed. (Chichester: Wiley Blackwell, 2022).

Alison Milbank, *Chesterton and Tolkien as Theologians: The Fantasy of the Real* (London: T. and T. Clark, 2007).

Brian Rosebury, *Tolkien: A Cultural Phenomenon* (Basingstoke: Palgrave Macmillan, 2003).

Tom Shippey, *J. R. R. Tolkien: Author of the Century* (London: HarperCollins, 2000).

Tom Shippey, *Roots and Branches: Selected Papers on Tolkien* (Zurich: Walking Tree, 2007).

Ross Smith, *Inside Language: Linguistic and Aesthetic Theory in Tolkien* (Zurich: Walking Tree, 2011).

Anna Vaninskaya, *Fantasies of Time and Death: Dunsany, Eddison, Tolkien* (London: Palgrave Macmillan, 2020).

Elizabeth Whittingham, *The Evolution of Tolkien's Mythology: A Study of the History of Middle-earth* (Jefferson, NC: McFarland and Co., 2008).

Toby Widdicombe, *J. R. R. Tolkien: A Guide for the Perplexed* (London: Bloomsbury Academic, 2020).

Index

For the benefit of digital users, indexed terms that span two pages (e.g., 52–3) may, on occasion, appear on only one of those pages.

Index

Index

BESTSELLERS
A Very Short Introduction
John Sutherland

'I rejoice', said Doctor Johnson, 'to concur with the Common Reader.' For the last century, the tastes and preferences of the common reader have been reflected in the American and British bestseller lists, and this *Very Short Introduction* takes an engaging look through the lists to reveal what we have been reading - and why. John Sutherland shows that bestseller lists monitor one of the strongest pulses in modern literature and are therefore worthy of serious study. Along the way, he lifts the lid on the bestseller industry, examines what makes a book into a bestseller, and asks what separates bestsellers from canonical fiction.

'His amiable trawl through the history of popular books is frequently entertaining'

Scott Pack, The Times

BIOGRAPHY
A Very Short Introduction
Hermione Lee

Biography is one of the most popular, best-selling, and
widely-read of literary genres. But why do certain people and
historical events arouse so much interest? How can biographies
be compared with history and works of fiction? Does a biography
need to be true? Is it acceptable to omit or conceal things? Does
the biographer need to personally know the subject? Must a
biographer be subjective? In this *Very Short Introduction*
Hermione Lee considers the cultural and historical background
of different types of biographies, looking at the factors that affect
biographers and whether there are different strategies, ethics,
and principles required for writing about one person compared to
another. She also considers contemporary biographical
publications and considers what kind of 'lives' are the most
popular and in demand.

> 'It would be hard to think of anyone better to provide a crisp
> contribution to OUP's Very Short Introductions.'

> **Kathryn Hughes, The Guardian**

CHILDREN'S LITERATURE
A Very Short Introduction
Kimberley Reynolds

Children's literature is vast and amorphous subject. From picture books and pop ups, to online games and eBooks, children's literature takes many forms.

In this energetic *Very Short Introduction,* Kim Reynolds details what children's literature is, why it's interesting, how it contributes to culture, and how it is studied. Reynolds considers how children's literature has helped to shape and direct ideas about culture, society and childhood as well as exploring how far negative depictions of the future for children may contribute to a lack of social vision. She raises questions about what shape the future of literature for children should take, and explores the crossover between children's literature and adult fiction.

www.oup.com/vsi